By the same author

Ruminations on College Life
Ruminations on Twentysomething Life
I'm Having More Fun Than You

LEXAPROS AND CONS

Aaron Karo

FARRAR STRAUS GIROUX
NEW YORK

Farrar Straus Giroux Books for Young Readers
175 Fifth Avenue, New York 10010

Copyright © 2012 by Aaron Karo
All rights reserved
Distributed in Canada by D&M Publishers, Inc.
Printed in the United States of America
Designed by Becky Terhune
First edition, 2012
1 3 5 7 9 10 8 6 4 2

macteenbooks.com

Library of Congress Cataloging-in-Publication Data
Karo, Aaron.
    Lexapros and cons / Aaron Karo. — 1st ed.
      p.   cm.
    Summary: Realizing that his OCD (obsessive-compulsive disorder) is out
of control, seventeen-year-old Chuck Taylor, who wants to win his best
friend back and impress a new girl at school, tries to break some hardcore
habits, face his demons—and get messy.
    ISBN: 978-0-374-34396-5
    [1. Obsessive-compulsive disorder—Fiction.   2. Interpersonal
relations—Fiction.]   I. Title.

PZ7.K1447Le 2012
[E]—dc23

                                                        2011022983

A12006 158525

For Caryn

In the past year, I masturbated exactly 468 times. That's an average of 9 times a week and 1.28 per day. I'm not sure what impresses me more, though—the fact that I jerk off so much, or the fact that I actually kept a running tally for an entire year. But I did. On a growing stack of Post-its in the drawer of my nightstand. Jerk off, make a note of it, go to sleep, routine.

The thing is, routines make up a huge part of my life. Okay, well, maybe "routines" isn't the right word. I know the right word now, but for a while I didn't. Basically what happened was that on January 1st of last year, I jerked off. For some unknown, unexplainable reason, I thought to my-self, *I wonder how many times I do this in a year?* Of course, the proper thought process for a typical, red-blooded teenager would be, *I should get a girlfriend, that way I won't have to jerk off so much.* But for whatever reason that's not the first thought that popped into my head.

My problem wasn't January 1st, though, it was January

2nd, when I jerked off again, and then made a note of it. Once I start doing something, no matter how idiotic, I can't stop. It's all I can think about. I tried to halt the tally in mid-March but then I couldn't sleep in that post-wank, pre-checkmark state, thinking, *Why not just keep the list going? You've made it so far!* Then I would make the tally, feel better, and then get up to pee. I also pee a lot.

The weird thing about all my "routines" is that I'm acutely aware of how crazy they are. It's not normal to get up to pee fifteen times before going to bed. I know I just peed, there could not possibly be any more urine in my bladder. I'm not gonna piss the bed; everything will be fine. But then I start to think about it until I can't help jumping out of bed and going to the bathroom. It's like if you start thinking about swallowing or breathing or blinking. Then that becomes the only thing you can think about. But eventually you forget. That's like me and peeing, except I never forget and it happens every single night. So I pee a lot.

I've got a few other bad "habits." The stove—well, the stove is a fucking nightmare. If I don't check the burner thingies, I'm convinced the house is gonna burn down with me, my sister, and my parents inside. When the stove is on, a little light goes on to alert you. But what if the light breaks? There are four burner thingies; you could theoretically walk past the stove and not realize that one of the knobs wasn't set to Off. Then, let's say a dish towel fell off the refrigerator handle (which is all the way across the kitchen, but let's just say), it landed on the burner, caught fire, and the entire Taylor family died in a horrible burner-thingy accident. I'm consumed by this thought. So I check the burners and the knobs by hand. Over and over. Several times a day. My parents barely even use the stove. I masturbate more than they cook.

The thing that really got me, though, was the hand washing. That's when I started to think, *Man, maybe you have a problem.* If my hands are dirty, I absolutely have to wash them. But my definition of dirty and your definition of dirty are probably very different. You probably wash your hands after you eat chicken wings or take a shit. I *must* wash my hands after touching animals, small children, public mailboxes, elevator buttons, money (especially coins), other people's hands, all food (plus salt, pepper, and condiments), and anything I consider "natural" (grass, dirt, wood, etc.). I wash my hands a lot. Sometimes it's the only thing I can think about.

Like I said, the hand washing is what first got me. If you Google "I keep track of how often I masturbate," you're not gonna get a lot of hits. Well, you'll get a boatload of hits—just not anything relevant or appropriate to be displayed in a high school computer lab. But if you Google "I can't stop washing my hands," it's a whole different story. Most of the results will point to one thing. What I do are not "routines." They're compulsions. You know when you read something and you're just like, *Fuck, that's me!* Well once I read this thing, I knew I had it.

My name is Chuck. I'm seventeen years old. And according to Wikipedia, I have OCD.

My name isn't actually Chuck. It's Charles. Why anyone would ever name a baby Charles I've never figured out. It's like my parents were living in nineteenth-century England or something. I'm named after my mom's grandfather, who she claims was a real intimidating guy. He died way before I was born, so we never met, but how badass can you be if your name is Charles? Fortunately, no one actually calls me Charles. I go by Chuck. That's what everyone at school calls me. Though, I guess "everyone" is relative. I'm pretty much invisible at school. Let's just say that's what my teachers and my one friend call me. Whatever. It's better than Charles.

Perhaps you've picked up on it by now (but probably you haven't)—my full name is Chuck Taylor. And unlike my great-grandfather, there is a Chuck Taylor in history who *definitely* was a badass. This Chuck Taylor was a basketball player in the 1920s. He worked for Converse and eventually had their most popular shoe named after him—the super-famous Chuck Taylor All Star. People call them Chucks or Cons and when I first saw a pair I thought it was the coolest thing ever. I mean, it's got my name right on the side! Soon, though, like everything else in my life, Cons became an obsession.

My mom was actually thrilled when I told her I wanted my first pair of Cons a few years ago. I had never really given the sneakers much thought until my best friend Steve found a Chuck Taylor biography in the school library. It only took a few pages for me to realize that I was destined to wear Cons. Chuck Taylor, that dude in *Grease*, Kurt Cobain, and then Chuck Taylor again. I loved the symmetry. Symmetry makes my brain feel nice.

When my mom found out I wanted $45 sneakers to replace the $85 ones I had worn out, she was more than willing. She actually bought me a few pairs—all high-tops because the low-tops don't have my name on them, and always solid colors because, well, I don't know . . . they just seem cleaner looking to me. My mom knew I had a thing for Cons and she encouraged it. Anything I got into, as long as it wasn't drugs (sharing the same pipe with six other people? Please!), she encouraged. There wasn't much. I guess when your only son is a nutcase who touches the stove more than you do, you'll do anything to put a smile on his face. I built a nice little Converse collection out of that pity.

But there's only so many sneakers a kid can have, even at $45 a pop, and Mom stopped buying them for me, so I had to dip into my savings account. I had some money in there from bonds I got when I was born and also from what passes as my weekly allowance. I could buy a pair of Cons every month just from that, and pretty soon I had amassed a mountain of them in my closet—every solid color available. And that's when things got weird.

Here's the thing. I'm not shy, it's just that no one really gives a shit about what I have to say (besides Steve and Mom, who don't count). So I'm quiet. But I'd rather be shy. Shy and quiet are different. Shy means you can't speak up. Quiet means you don't want to. This past summer was especially rough because Steve went away with his parents for like two months. It was just me and my Cons, stuck in Plainville with nothing to do. The only one who ever asked me how I was feeling was Mom, who, again, doesn't count.

Now I've always kept the closet in my bedroom so organized you'd probably hesitate before touching anything in it—like it's a museum (which is sorta the point). However, my method for choosing which Cons to wear was actually quite haphazard—I'd grab whatever pair struck my fancy that day and run out the door. But haphazardness, as you might imagine, is generally not something I can tolerate for long. One morning, I walked in on my younger sister Beth using my laptop—which she knows she's not allowed to do. I yelled at her but she just ignored me and walked out of my room. Beth is brilliant at ignoring me. Worst sister ever. I was angry. I grabbed my red Cons. On my way out the door, Mom asked how I was feeling. I said, "Fine."

Somewhere, deep in my brain, deep down in a synapse, a neuron fired. *Angry = red Cons.* The next day, I was more tired than anything. The red Cons were still there of course, but I wasn't angry anymore. I chose the orange

Cons instead. *Tired = orange*. And so my system was born. Whatever I was feeling that morning would determine which sneakers I wore that day. The colors themselves didn't make much sense—orange and tired really have no connection—but the connection was made in my head. And just like with the stove-checking or my masturbation tally, once a connection is made in my head, I can't break it. So instead of expressing myself like a normal kid, I began using my Cons as a kind of shorthand. Every day, a different mood, a different color. A little threat-level advisory code of my emotions. Except no one—not even Steve—realized what I was doing.

III

Steve and I hang out a lot in his basement, mostly playing video games.

"Did you see *Sensual Moon III* last night on Skinemax?" Steve asks.

"There's a *Sensual Moon III*? I didn't even know there was a *Sensual Moon II*," I respond.

Steve is really into those softcore porn movies they play on cable late at night. He goes to sleep, then sets an alarm to wake up in three hours and turn on the TV.

"Hell yeah there was a *Sensual Moon II*; that was the best one!"

Steve loves Skinemax. Even though every guy in the universe uses the Internet for porn, Steve refers to himself as a "masturbatory traditionalist." He likes the production values on Skinemax. Steve is a fucking weirdo. Which is probably why we get along.

I first met him in fourth grade when his family moved to Plainville. Since Steve was new, he didn't have any friends.

And even though I had lived here all my life, I didn't either. We've been best friends ever since.

"No, I didn't see it. Skinemax is usually blocked in my room," I say.

"Oh man, it was great. There's much dirtier stuff online, but *Sensual Moon* is just *classy*. Reminds me of—"

"That time you got a hand job?"

"Yeah, that was awesome."

Last summer, when Steve was traveling with his parents to all the biggest national parks in the country, he claims he got a hand job from a girl in California. This supposed hand job is the high point of his life and he does not stop talking about it. I guess I don't blame him. He doesn't have much else to be psyched about. Like me, Steve has a somewhat unusual name—Steve Sludgelacker. But while I have the same name as a famous basketball player, Steve's name happens to rhyme with "fudge packer." The bullies at school tend to remind him of that every day. With their fists. So I never really bug him for the details of the hand job, even though the story seems dubious. He has enough to deal with.

It's winter break and we still have a few days off before heading back for the second half of our senior year. Luckily, me and Steve both got into college Early Decision. High school graduation is only six months away, which means we are that much closer to leaving for college, which means we are that much closer to getting the hell out of Plainville. But it also means we are that much closer to leaving high school as pathetic virgins. I've never had a girlfriend. And Steve, well, I guess Steve has his hand job.

"Damn it. Killed again," Steve says. We're playing this new game where you're the zombies and you get to shoot the soldiers, instead of the other way around. Pretty sweet, unless you keep getting killed like Steve does. "Stupid game," he says as he hits Reset. "So I was at Applebee's last night with my parents. Stacey Simpson was there."

"Oh yeah?" I offer.

Stacey is the hottest girl in our class. It's not even close. "Blonde with cannons" is how Steve describes her. In fact, I'd say she's the source material I used to fantasize about one-third of the tallies on last year's jerk-off list. We were actually partners (not her choosing) in eighth-grade Home Ec, and she watched as I scrubbed my hands any time even a morsel of food touched them. Within a week she asked to switch partners, and never acknowledged my existence again. Luckily, I have plenty of stock footage stored up.

"Chuck, I'm telling you, Stacey's tits grew over winter break. They're like fucking cantaloupes."

"No way," I say.

"Something was different. She is so hot."

"Did you talk to her?"

Steve continues playing without responding to my question. It's not necessary. Of course he didn't talk to her. We aren't the type to talk to hot girls. Or any girls for that matter. Sometimes I wish me and Steve were nerdier. There's a lot of nerds in Plainville—at least we'd have a clique. But the nerds are all *really* nerdy. They do calculus for fun and play ridiculous role-playing games online for like fifteen hours at a time. So here me and Steve are—stuck in the lonely region between the jocks and the nerds. Sadly, we're neither athletes nor mathletes.

"So when I was in California—"

"Can we talk about something else besides your hand job?"

Even though it's freezing outside, I walk home from Steve's because he only lives two blocks away. I step on some of the cracks in the sidewalk as I go. It doesn't bother me. Besides washing your hands, avoiding cracks on the sidewalk seems to be the most common trait they give a character with OCD on television or in a movie. But I don't care about whether or not I step on a crack. That just isn't one of my "things." I have no idea why I'm okay with it. It's almost annoying in a weird way.

I wave hello to our senile old neighbors the Greulichs, who are sitting on their front porch being senile and old, then walk into my house. Mom is cooking, which is unusual. I say a quick hello and make a mental note that there will have to be some extra stove-checking tonight. I go downstairs to the living room where my dad is watching some NBA pregame show on TV. My grandpa Sam, who died last year, was a huge basketball fan. Me: not so much. With Grandpa gone, I don't think Dad has anyone to talk to about sports, and I think he hopes I'll fill that void. Unfortunately, my connection with basketball begins and ends with the fact that the guy whose sneakers I wear played it eighty years ago.

"Big game?" I ask.

"As big a game as there can be at this point in the season," Dad says.

I don't understand, and Dad realizes as much.

"The playoffs don't start until April."

"Oh," I say, "right."

Dad eyes my Cons. They're pink. Before I went to Steve's house, I was pretty bored. Pink happens to mean bored in my system, so I tend to wear pink Cons a lot. This does not sit well with my dad. He never actually says anything, but I suspect that he suspects I'm gay. I mean, I've never even had a *girl friend*—space in between. And I wear pink sneakers sometimes. I almost don't blame Dad for thinking that. But I'm definitely not gay. Just terrible around girls. And really fucking bored.

"The trading deadline is coming soon; these guys are playing for their jobs," Dad remarks.

I nod in agreement as if this means anything to me.

"Also, me and Mom want to talk to you before dinner."

"About what?" I ask.

"She'll tell you. It's no big deal. When do you go back to school again?"

It actually amuses me that my dad kinda gets pissed whenever I'm off from school. Sometimes I just want to say, "Dad, I'm seventeen. You're forty-seven. What do you want me to do?"

"I go back Monday. You know that."

"Just seems like a really long break. *I'm* still working."

Dad is an accountant. Now don't get me wrong, I'm good at math. I'm in Calc AB, which is the second highest class you can possibly be in. In fact, if I do well on the AP test in May, I could even get college credit for it. But I still hate calculus. I can't believe my dad's actual job is to do math all day. Math for other people. Not only does it sound awful, but it's one less thing we have in common. Steve's dad's company makes the plastic casing that video games come in. At least that's sorta kinda cool.

"You're working this week because you're *old*, Dad!" I say. I'm joking. Despite our cavernous differences, me and Dad still joke around a lot, and I love that. He smiles.

"Not too old to come over there and smack ya," he says. Also joking.

Just as the game is about to start, Mom calls down from the kitchen. *"Chuck! Ray!"* Mind you the kitchen and the living room are not that far away.

"Coming!" we respond simultaneously, yelling just as loudly as Mom had. But we don't go upstairs for another few minutes. Dad wants to see if he can catch tip-off. I remember I touched a twig on the way home from Steve's and go to wash my hands.

In fact, when I finally walk into the kitchen, Dad hasn't even come upstairs yet. Mom is making pasta shells, one of my favorites (in part because I won't have to use my hands)—but also an unusual move that's starting to make me suspicious.

"Where's Dad?" she asks.

"Probably still watching the game. Where's Beth?"

My sister is a sophomore, so we've already spent a year and a half together in high school. I bet if you polled all 1,600 students, 99 percent would know who she is and about 1 percent would know who I am. That 99 percent figure is a conservative estimate, assuming she's unknown to the sixteen or so mathletes who only talk to each other. My 1 percent figure is a generous estimate, assuming there's some kids who only know me because I'm Beth's older brother. There's a reason, though, behind this disparity. Two reasons actually. I'm only going to mention them this one time and then never, ever speak of them again. Beth's got big boobs. Next topic.

"She's in her room," Mom says.

I know what Beth is doing in there. Popular-girl stuff. Someone posts on her Facebook Wall every fifteen seconds. She has yet to respond to my friend request.

"Will you call your dad again?" Mom asks.

"Dad!" I yell.

My dad always jokes that he's the president of our house in name only. It's really Mom who's the chief executive officer. And he's right. Mom's a teacher (though thankfully she teaches elementary school and didn't work when I was younger; if she had ever been *my* teacher I think I would have died of embarrassment). But I really think she should be a detective instead. She asks *so* many questions.

"How was Steve's?"

"Fine."

"What did you guys do?"

"Nothing."

"Nothing?"

"Played video games or whatever."

"What game?"

"Does it matter what game, Mom?"

Mom herself is kinda like that movie *Tron*: as soon as she is about to hit a wall, she changes directions.

"Are you ready to go back to school?"

"No."

"You're not excited for graduation?"

"I guess."

"You should start thinking about what you're gonna need for your dorm room."

"Okay."

"Also, I was thinking we could have a graduation party. You know, in the backyard. What do you think?"

"I don't know, maybe."

I sit down and pour myself some soda. A few months ago, I told Mom that I looked up obsessive-compulsive disorder on Wikipedia. In hindsight, that was probably a mistake. Mom and Dad knew about some of my rituals and habits, but I think they either chalked it up to teenage weirdness or were just in denial about how serious it might actually be. As soon as I brought it up, though, Mom started saying how OCD runs in the family, and that her dad had it, and that she thinks she might have had some symptoms when she was a teenager, *blah blah blah.* So for the past few months, Mom has been worried about me. I hate when Mom worries about me. Not only does it make me feel bad, but it also invites more questions. She knows having a graduation party means it would only be me, Steve, and her and Dad's friends. *"What do you think about having a graduation party?"* in Mom-speak translates to: *"Maybe if you weren't so OCD, you'd have more friends to invite to this mythical party we're not actually gonna have."* She's worried. And relentless.

"Are those new sneakers?" she asks.

"Nope, you've seen them like a thousand times."

"Oh, they seem different."

"They're exactly the same as all the other ones. Jesus, Mom."

Another wall.

Mom comes over and kisses me on the forehead. Crisis defused. Then she yells right in my ear.

"Ray! Come upstairs!"

No way," I say. "Absolutely not." I immediately feel my face go red and hot and feel like I'm gonna cry, which is the worst feeling because the more you think about it, the more you almost do actually cry.

The "no big deal" conversation my dad was referring to is the fact that my parents want me to see a psychiatrist.

"We're worried about you," Mom says, confirming what I already know. "We feel like your symptoms are getting worse. We want you to talk to someone. What if you're suffering from depression?"

"I'm fine, Mom."

"You're not fine. We just want to help," she says.

"Dad!" I plead.

As much as they try to put up a united front, Dad is easier to crack. But right now he's playing it safe.

"Listen to your mother."

The thing is, my mom is usually right. If I really think back on everything she's ever told me or advised me to do,

I can't come up with one example of her being wrong. Last time me and Steve went to the movies, I told her we were gonna leave at 7:30. She said to leave at 7:15 just in case it sold out. We got the last tickets. What colleges to apply to, which laptop to buy, whether milk's gone bad—right, right, and right. She is never wrong. And, deep down, I know she's right about this, too. On one hand, I'm pretty normal. I don't cut myself or throw up after I eat or listen to Marilyn Manson with a rope tied around my neck. On the other hand, I have to turn the lock on my school locker exactly fourteen times before walking away, I check myself for ticks every time I brush against a blade of grass, and, for the love of God, I counted how many times I jerked off for an entire year.

"One of the teachers at my school gave me the name of an excellent psychiatrist," Mom says. "Just go once. That's all we're asking."

Sometimes I daydream about being free from my compulsions. Not having to walk the same exact route every day in school. Touching the food in the cafeteria with my hands. But I'm still not ready to *talk* to someone about it.

"And if you like her," Mom continues, "you just have to go once a week—for an hour. Fifty minutes actually."

"Let's not get ahead of ourselves, Molly," Dad says. "We still don't know if insurance is gonna cover this."

I have three inner monologues going at once. One is freaking out about having to talk to someone about all my craziness, most of which my parents aren't even aware of. The second is actually kinda secretly hoping to be able to talk to someone about all my craziness. And the third is laughing at my dad, who is less concerned with his mentally ill son and more concerned about how much it's gonna cost.

"Ray . . ." my mom says, giving Dad the death stare. He stops talking immediately and looks at his feet. Mom turns to me.

"Honey, remember when you showed me that Flickapedia article about OCD and I said that—"

"Wikipedia."

"What?"

"Mom, it's Wikipedia. Not Flickapedia."

"Sorry, Wikipedia. Do you remember when you showed me that article?"

"Yes."

I never should have showed her that article.

"Chuck, I think that might have been a cry for help."

A cry for what? Seriously, Mom?

"I've been doing some research since then," she says, "and I think you're right. You probably have obsessive-compulsive disorder. And that's great."

"How the hell is that great?"

"Because now we know what's wrong and you can get treatment."

"But I don't wanna see a psychiatrist."

I'm starting to tear up. Goddamnit. This just makes my mom more upset, my dad more uncomfortable, and me feel more like a pussy.

"Chuck, it's okay," Dad says. "Just give it a try. I'll take you. I'll sit there in the waiting room. If you never want to go back again, you don't have to. And afterwards we can go to GameStop."

My nose is fucking running.

"A lot of people see shrinks," he adds. "I even saw one after Grandpa died."

I Googled it later, and apparently "shrink" is short for "head-shrinker," which is literally what these tribes in the Amazon do to skulls to make them into trophies and stuff. Somewhere along the way, it became slang for "therapist." Appropriate, I think.

So now my dad is both bribing me with video games and telling me he's seen a shrink, too. Well played, Dad.

"Okay," I sniffle.

"Okay?" Mom asks.

"Yes. Can I have a tissue?"

Dad takes out one of the handkerchiefs that he always carries around and holds it on my nose so that all I have to do is blow. Then he folds it up and puts it back in his pocket.

"Gross, Dad!"

We all share a snicker and I wipe my eyes. It's official: Chuck Taylor is going to see a shrink.

Beth comes bounding down the stairs, just in time for pasta shells.

"What are you guys talking about?" she asks, as always completely oblivious.

Rocking yellow Cons today: nervous. Inside a glass case hanging on the wall of the lobby is a listing of all the medical offices in the building. I see my shrink first because she has the longest name:

> ### DR. AHLADITA SRINIVASAN
> ### CHILD AND ADOLESCENT THERAPY

I have a little of that upset feeling in my stomach. Dad walks behind me, perhaps, I suspect, because he thinks I'm gonna make a run for it.

Dr. Srinivasan's office is on the thirteenth floor, which is both A) kind of ironic considering she deals with nutcases all day and B) not that big a deal because the number thirteen isn't one of my "things." I always think it's stupid that some buildings don't have a thirteenth floor because it's unlucky. It's just a number. (Says the guy with the masturbation tally.)

Me and Dad get into the elevator but I don't press the button even though I'm standing closest. Elevator buttons *are* one of my "things." You know how disgusting they are? How many people pick their nose and then press their floor? I take a step back. Dad sighs then reaches over and hits the button. He isn't as good as Mom is about remembering what my things are.

The waiting room is small and, thankfully, empty. It kind of looks like the study a superhero would have. Everything is brown and plain, but I imagine if you pulled one of the books on the shelf, a secret lair would open up behind the fish tank. There's a few little plastic kiddy chairs in one corner and stacks of ragged magazines on the coffee table, like *Highlights*, *Time for Kids*, and *American Girl*. How old are the people who come here? Can you be nine and be depressed?

Thinking it will impress Dad, I grab a regular, not-for-kids *Sports Illustrated*, but it turns out to be two years old. Ahladita Srinivasan needs newer magazines.

We only wait a few minutes before the door to the office itself opens, and Dr. Srinivasan comes out with a really tall girl. Like, *really* tall. I'm average height for a seventeen-year-old and Beth is a little taller than me. This girl is taller than Beth. Maybe that's this girl's problem: tallness. She walks right past us. I figure she's about my age. And since she doesn't have anyone waiting there to pick her up, she must have driven herself. Suddenly I feel really stupid sitting there with my dad.

Dr. Srinivasan looks like a pear. She's got a tiny little head and the rest of her body just expands from there. Two things about her I totally predicted: she wears glasses and she has lots of jewelry around her neck. That's straight out of the Indian psychiatrist playbook. The one thing I didn't expect: she's wearing sneakers. Those kind of old-school, low-top Nikes that are sort of suede. Blue with a yellow swoosh. I'm a Converse man myself, of course, but I respect the choice.

"You must be Chuck Taylor?" she says to me, as me and Dad stand up.

My dad speaks first.

"I'm Ray, Chuck's dad. You spoke to my wife, Molly, on the phone."

"Yes, of course. It's wonderful to meet you both. Chuck, why don't you come in and have a seat? Mr. Taylor, please make yourself comfortable and enjoy a magazine?"

I take one last look at Dad before trudging inside. Dr. Srinivasan's office is like a much more modern version of the waiting room. It smells like new carpet with a dash of cinnamon. Sitting on a shelf is one of those electronic sound machine things. I think it's on babbling-brook mode. There are two leather chairs. Between them is a coffee table. On that table is a box of tissues. It's empty. That doesn't seem good. We sit down.

"How are you today, Chuck?"

I look her in the eye for the first time. "Okay, I guess."

"The first thing I want to tell you is that everything we talk about in here is confidential? Unless there are extraordinary circumstances in which I feel you are in danger, anything you tell me stays in this room? Do you understand?"

Dr. Srinivasan has a thick accent, which, I quickly realize, goes up at the end of some of her sentences, so that it seems like she's asking a question even when she's not.

"Chuck? This is important?"

"Sorry . . . are you asking me if I understand, or if this is important?

"If you understand, yes?"

"Yeah, I understand."

She crosses her legs and places a small notepad on her lap. I still can't believe she's wearing sneakers and a dress. So weird.

"Typically, Chuck, during my first session, I do what is known as an 'intake.' All that means is that I get some background information about you so that we can better work together to help you?"

"Yes," I say instinctively.

"Excuse me?"

"Oh, sorry. I wasn't sure if that was a question."

She just smiles. "So, Chuck, tell me about yourself?"

Despite the fact that no one has ever asked me that in my entire life—which is kinda sad I must say—I have absolutely no desire to spill my guts to some stranger. I clam up.

"It's okay, Chuck," she says, tapping her pen on the notepad. "Start wherever you'd like?"

It's gonna be a long fifty minutes . . .

Unfortunately, Monday has finally arrived. Steve is driving me to school in his used powder blue Ford Taurus. My parents won't buy me a car, but apparently the video game plastic-casing business is quite lucrative for the Sludgelackers.

"So how long did you sit there?" Steve asks.

"Like half an hour."

"Without saying anything?"

"I mean, she said, 'Tell me about yourself.' What was I supposed to say?"

"I don't know. You're a neat freak. You have more shoes than Carrie Bradshaw."

"Carrie Bradshaw?"

"Yeah, you know, from *Sex and the City*?"

"Steve, you're a fucking weirdo."

"Hey, I'm not the one seeing a shrink."

We crawl through Plainville on the way to school. The streets are snowy and icy, and Steve's Taurus doesn't exactly have four-wheel drive. Plainville is the standard kind of suburb where every house looks pretty much the same. When they're covered by snow, though, every house looks identical. God I want to leave this place.

"So are you gonna go back?" Steve asks.

"Huh?"

"To the shrink. Are you gonna go back to the shrink?"

"Psychiatrist. I don't know. I doubt my dad is gonna take me to GameStop after every session."

"I can't believe you got three new games. My dad makes all the cases and he still doesn't hook me up with anything. I wish I was crazy. You're definitely coming over after school to play."

"Yeah, well," I continue, "I guess we did talk about some stuff toward the end of the session. I told her how annoying Beth is."

"Really? What else did you tell her about Beth?"

Steve is in love with Beth. Ever since we were in ninth grade and Beth was in seventh, he's been obsessed with her. It's worse than when he talks about his hand job because this . . . this is my fucking sister. He asks me to set him up with her about once a week. Seriously? No. And it's not like I have any sway with Beth anyway. Besides, Beth thinks Steve is a total dork. She hasn't told me this outright, but I kind of assumed it when I informed her that Steve had offered to give her a ride to school every day and she said she'd *rather take the bus.*

"I don't remember what I told her exactly," I say. "Mostly that Beth's annoying and I hate her."

"Come on. Beth isn't annoying. She's a lovely . . . blossoming young woman."

"Steve, what did I say about talking about my sister? I *will* kill you."

"Not if Parker gets me first."

We drive in silence for a while. Parker Goldberg is the captain of the Plainville soccer team and Steve's nemesis. Although, I think "nemesis" isn't really the right word. It implies that Parker is the villain in a comic book that Steve does battle with. In reality, it's a little more one-sided. Parker is a bully who Steve is powerless to stop. It was Parker who, on Steve's first day of school in fourth grade, shouted out "Fudge Packer!" as soon as he was introduced to the class. Steve looks like a short, pale Milhouse from *The Simpsons* (without the glasses), so he's already an easy target, but Parker has tormented him every day since. Sometimes verbally, sometimes physically, and sometimes he just steals Steve's lunch money, which is fucking ridiculous. Who actually steals lunch money? It sounds like it's from a bad *Saved by the Bell* rerun. At least be original, Parker.

I change the subject. "So what do you think Senior Weekend is gonna be?"

"I heard it's gonna be paintball," Steve says.

"There's no way it's gonna be paintball. But that *would* be awesome."

Senior Weekend is literally the only thing I'm looking forward to between now and college. It takes place at the end of the school year, a couple of weeks before prom. Student government decides on the location and, even though it's not officially sanctioned by the school, it's a tradition that's gone on for so long that they kinda just look the other way. Basically, it's just an overnight trip somewhere. But the sweet part is that it's the only time the entire senior class gets together for a non-school event. The nerds go, the popular kids go, and even me and Steve will go. One year it was laser tag. Last year it was to an amusement park. The location is always kept secret until it's announced before first period on the first day back after winter break. I'm not gonna lie: I'm super excited. I do not wear my blue Cons very often, but today I'm rocking them proudly.

We pull into the parking lot. Our town is adjacent to a much smaller town called West Lake, and kids from both towns go to one school: Plainville–West Lake JFK. Written out completely, it's Plainville–West Lake John Fitzgerald Kennedy High School. Longest school name in American history. It has been the site of many indignities for me and Steve. But today, the PWLJFKHS senior parking lot is buzzing with anticipation.

S teve's right: Stacey Simpson's tits *do* look bigger. As president of the senior class, she's standing onstage in the school auditorium with the rest of student government. The other kids in our class have also arrived early before first period, and we're all milling about, waiting for the announcement. Steve catches me gawking at Stacey.

"I told you," he whispers. "Cantaloupes."

What I wouldn't give to see Stacey naked. Or any girl for that matter who isn't streaming on a free porn site. Despite my best efforts not to, I just began my masturbation tally again on January 1st. I don't know why I'm compelled to keep track of it. *What is wrong with me?* And to make matters worse, I'm already beating (no pun intended) last year's pace. Now Stacey is jumping up and down with glee upon seeing one of her girl friends. *Whoa.* At least I have some new material in case the Internet goes down.

Me and Steve are both mesmerized, but that trance is soon interrupted when Parker arrives. He's almost exactly my size, but just *cut*. And no matter what the weather or occasion, he *always always always* wears those warm-up pants with the snaps that go all the way up the sides. When I've half watched an NBA game with my dad, I've seen the players wear the same ones on the bench, and then just rip them off before they go into the game. I guess they're sorta cool—if you're in the NBA.

Parker walks by, roughly elbows Steve, mutters, "Welcome back, Fudge Packer," then casually strolls away toward the rest of the soccer jocks, all in one fluid motion. He's one multitasking bully.

Steve seems to take it in stride (as always) but I feel powerless to help. I feel even more awful because Parker completely ignores me. I almost want him to hit *me*. At least then I could commiserate with Steve—and have someone in this school actually notice me. Steve rubs his arm. Then again, maybe it's better to be ignored. We sit.

Stacey finally struts to the microphone on the stage as the four hundred or so seniors wait with bated breath in front of the auditorium.

"Hello, everybody!" she chirps. "As you all know, today is the day when the location of Senior Weekend is revealed."

Everyone cheers and whistles.

"I'm thrilled to announce that this year, Senior Weekend will be a camping trip! We'll be camping overnight at the Randall Kaufman campgrounds in West Lake. There's gonna be bonfires and s'mores . . . and *beverages*. So get those sleeping bags and tents ready because it's gonna be a blast!"

My heart sinks. That feeling like just before you're about to go on the big drop on a roller coaster. Camping? *Fucking camping?*

All the other seniors are thrilled. They hoot and holler

and slap each other five and brag about what kind of alcohol they're gonna bring, even though the trip is five months away. I sit in my seat and don't move.

Camping is my worst-case scenario. The equivalent of an asteroid hitting Earth and the resulting debris blocking out the sun and killing all the dinosaurs. Being outdoors—sleeping outdoors!—for two days? Grass? Dirt? No showers? Bugs? Maybe some weird snakes or something? Eating messy s'mores with no place to wash up? Going to the bathroom in a porta-potty . . . *or in the bushes?* This is a nightmare. An absolute nightmare.

My face starts to get red and hot again. Thankfully most of the class is already filing out. Steve is still sitting next to me, unclear what the problem is.

"I'm not going," I say resolutely.

"What?" he says.

"I'm not going camping."

"Why not?"

"I don't know. It's just not my thing."

"You've been talking about this since freshman year."

"Whatever, it's not that big a deal."

"Not that big a deal? Wait. Is this because of your OCD thing?"

"No. I just don't like camping."

"Have you ever been?"

"No."

"Well, last summer—"

"I don't want to hear about your fucking hand job, Steve."

"I'm not talking about that. You know I went with my parents to all those national parks. We camped a couple of nights. It's awesome."

"I don't know. Maybe I'll think about it."

But I already know I'm not gonna go. Just the thought of it makes me want to wash my hands. It makes me sad. All I want to do is end school on a high note. Now even that's ruined. Why couldn't we have gone to a water park or something? Some place with *facilities*. Life really sucks sometimes.

"Well, if you don't go," Steve says, "then I won't go."

While it's a nice gesture, I know Steve won't go without me anyway. He's probably worried about getting beaten to a bloody pulp by Parker and left to die in the woods alone.

The first-period bell rings. It's time to continue my meager high school existence. College can't come soon enough.

"We'll talk about it later, Chuck. Most likely when we're playing your new video games in my basement after school."

I barely acknowledge him. I want to sit here until my face stops being so red.

Calc AB with Mr. Cimaglia is my first-period class. Thankfully, he hasn't started yet as I trudge in a minute late. I sit at my desk. Even my randomly assigned class seating ensures no one pays much attention to me—not too close to the front but not too far in the back either. Kanha Ramesh, a kid me and Steve eat lunch with, and the only other person in school I speak to on a semi-regular basis, sits a few rows back. I don't turn to say hello.

I stare at my blue Cons. The one drawback of my system is that I'm stuck with whichever ones I put on in the morning. Excited is the last thing I feel now.

I'm so preoccupied with that goddamn camping trip I barely notice that Principal Rodriguez has come to the door to talk to Mr. Cimaglia. When I finally look up again, I realize that Mr. Cimaglia is now standing in front of the class, introducing a new student.

I'm blindsided. I clutch the sides of my desk like it's about to achieve flight. This girl, whoever she is, is beautiful.

She's about an inch shorter than me, with bright red bangs that pretty much cover her eyes. The next thing I notice is that she doesn't have any freckles. All the gingers I've ever met have had tons of freckles. But not her. Her skin is completely clear. She brushes the hair out of her blue eyes, but it keeps returning right back to where it started. She seems really uncomfortable standing up there. But who wouldn't be? And who the hell is she?

Mr. Cimaglia is so bald his scalp has a glare, and he speaks in total monotone. Listening to him is like when you enter something into an automated voice system and it repeats the number back to you all robotic-like. "Can I have your attention, please," he says. "Your attention, please. I'd like to introduce a new student who will be joining the class. This is Amy Huntington. She just moved here from San Diego. Please welcome her."

Amy. *Amy* . . .

Amy does kind of a half curtsy / half smile / half eye roll. Yeah, I know that's too many halves (and this is math class to boot), but that's the best way to describe it. She sits down—one row to the right of me and two seats ahead of me. She never even looks in my direction. It's hard to tell where she's looking with those bangs, but I'm positive she doesn't look in my direction. She's wearing those shoes that girls wear that look like ballet slippers. Usually pretty dumb. She pulls it off, though. *Who are you, Amy Huntington? And who changes high schools six months before graduation?*

Mr. Cimaglia begins the class. We're picking up where we left off before winter break, with antiderivatives. I understand them pretty well and find them incredibly boring (as usual), so I have a good opportunity to stare at Amy. When Mr. Cimaglia starts to write on the board, Amy opens up her notebook and realizes she doesn't have a pen. She looks upset. I have two pens. *Say something, Chuck. Say something!*

Wendy Perfit, the token brunette in Stacey's gaggle of pretty girls, notices and hands her one. I miss my chance like a moron. Amy smiles. Her smile . . . well, it makes *me* smile.

"Chuck? Chuck. Is something funny?"

Oh crap. Mr. Cimaglia catches me with a stupid, shit-eating grin on my face.

"No, Mr. Cimaglia. Sorry."

I look down in embarrassment, past my textbook, through the desk, and into the floor. Then I sneak a quick glance to see if Amy has looked back at me. But she just sits there facing straight ahead. She doesn't look back the entire class. Believe me, I would know if she did. I'm having that just-about-to-drop-on-a-roller-coaster feeling like before. But this time it's something different.

Amy brushes her hair out of her eyes again. I stifle another smile. Suddenly, Senior Weekend seems like the least important thing in the world.

Turns out I did wear the right Cons today after all.

After school, in Steve's basement, I do not shut up about Amy. At least now Steve understands how I feel about hearing about his hand job.

"How come no hot, mysterious girls come to my classes?" Steve says. "I knew I should have taken Calc with Cimaglia."

"I'm telling you, Steve," I say, "this is the girl I've been waiting for."

"Waiting for?"

"Yeah."

"Implying you have the capability to hook up with any girl at school but were just waiting for one in particular?"

I take out one of my new video games and taunt Steve with it.

"You *really* don't want to play this, do you?"

"Okay, okay, you win," he says. "So what are you gonna do? Are you gonna talk to her?"

Obviously not.

"Yes. I'm gonna talk to her."

"Really?"

No, not really.

"Definitely. I'm definitely gonna talk to her."

Steve wrinkles his forehead.

"I think you're gonna need a plan, Chuck."

"You're right. What should I do?"

"Well, what do we know about her?"

"Her hair gets in her eyes a lot," I say. I ponder this. Then I have a thought: "I could get her a headband or something!"

Steve just looks at me. "You're better than that," he says.

"Okay. Headband is a bad idea."

"What else?"

"Well, she seems to have a shortage of pens."

"Now we're talking," Steve says, grinning.

Today in Calc, I've come prepared—with like thirty pens. Ten black, ten blue, a pink one I stole from Beth, a couple of rollerballs thrown in for good measure, and even one of those giant pens where you can change the color it writes in. If Amy needs a pen, I'm her guy. There's only one problem, though: Amy isn't here. The bell rings and Mr. Cimaglia picks up the lesson (again with the fucking antiderivatives), but Amy's seat is empty. No joke: for a minute I think I've imagined the whole thing. Pretty girls don't just show up magically. Not in my life anyway. But then, out of nowhere (okay, the hallway), she appears.

"I'm sorry. I got lost," Amy says, as she scurries into the classroom. She seems frazzled and Mr. Cimaglia gives her a friendly smile.

"No problem. We were just getting started," he says.

Amy sits down and blows her bangs out of her eyes. She seems overheated—like she just jogged to class after getting turned around. I feel bad for her. What she really needs is a glass of cold water, and all I have are lots and lots of pens. Story of my life.

To add insult to injury, Amy already *has* a pen. And it's not the same one that Wendy gave her yesterday. So either she brought one from home, or she got another pen from someone else between yesterday's class and today's. I'm convinced it's the latter scenario. Which means Amy is having contact with other kids in school—kids who will quickly realize how awesome and pretty she is. Soon I'll have even less of a shot than the minuscule one I'm already clinging to. Time is not on my side.

"I still can't believe she already had a pen," I say to Steve, as he drives me home after school.

"Well, that *was* one of the risks we discussed with the pen strategy," he says.

It's a bullshit strategy and we both know it. I'm just stalling and Steve is enabling me.

"What if I friended her on Facebook?" I offer.

"Hmmm . . ." Steve ponders. "Is creepy and stalkerish the look you're going for?"

"How is that creepy and stalkerish?"

"Well, for one, she has no idea who you are. That's the creepy part. And friending someone you haven't actually spoken to in real life? That's the stalker part."

"She probably wouldn't even accept my request anyway," I say. "I mean, Beth hasn't."

"Beth hasn't accepted mine either."

"What?"

I don't think Steve meant to let that slip out.

"Why the fuck are you friending my sister?"

"It was a few months ago. Remember? We were at your house and Beth walked by and said, 'Hi, Steve.' It was a Tuesday."

"I do *not* remember that."

"Oh I remember it exactly. She said, 'Hi, Steve.' Just like that: *Hi, Steve.*"

"Okay, Jesus, I get it. So you felt that interaction warranted a friend request?"

"Chuck, we're not talking about me here. We're talking about Amy. Right?"

I'm fully aware that Steve is trying to change the subject on me. But Amy is my top priority.

"Right," I concede. "We're talking about Amy."

We continue home, Steve's Taurus barely getting any traction in the snow.

"You wanna hang out now?" he says. "We can figure out your next move."

"I can't. I have an appointment with Dr. S."

Since I went to the shrink last week, Mom has been hassling me to go back. I knew that was coming when I agreed to go in the first place. And although I haven't admitted it to Mom, I don't *hate* the idea of going back. Dr. S. is pretty nice, I guess. It's cool to have someone else who cares. Even if she's getting paid for it.

"Who the hell is Dr. S.?" Steve asks.

"Dr. Srinivasan. The psychiatrist. She told me to call her Dr. S."

"*Dr. S.* kinda sounds like that dermatologist who advertises on bus stops."

This was true.

"Whatever," I say, and leave it at that. "I'll text you afterwards."

We don't talk much the rest of the way home. I don't know what Steve is thinking, but every time we hit a patch of snow and the car bumps up and down, I can hear all the pens flying around in my backpack. Something tells me I'll need more than Bics to win Amy over.

I drive Mom's car to Dr. S.'s office this time. When I arrive, there's no patient before me. Maybe it's a slow day in the crazy business.

Dr. S. is wearing sneakers again. Thankfully, they're the same ones as last time. If my shrink had some sort of weird sneaker fetish, too, I'd freak out.

"I thought that our first session was successful?" Dr. S. says/asks. "I understand you are hesitant to share everything with me at first. This is normal. I suggest that today we start to talk a little bit about your symptoms, yes?"

"Like, my routines?"

"Exactly. Your routines. What kinds of things do you do?"

I take a deep breath.

Here goes nothing.

"Well, I wash my hands a lot. Like, all the time. Even when they're not dirty."

Dr. S. nods.

"Um, I have this thing with the stove in my house. I

always have to check the burner thingies. Make sure they're not on."

"How do you make sure they're not on?"

"I touch them over and over again. I stare at the knobs. I listen for the gas . . . which is kinda ironic now that I think about it, since it's electric."

I chuckle at my own idiocy. Dr. S. barely smirks then makes a note in her little pad. For some reason, I imagine she's playing hangman and slowly spelling out N-U-T-C-A-S-E.

"Continue?"

"I also make a million lists. Like, To Do lists. Sometimes of stupid stuff, like 'make bed.' I make lists over and over again and then rewrite them for no reason."

I didn't always consider list making one of my things, but apparently it's a common OCD trait. Stupid Wikipedia. Now I'm self-conscious about it. Dr. S. nods again.

"I also have to knock on wood," I say.

Dr. S. looks confused, so I have to explain this one.

"If I have a bad thought, I have to knock on wood. You know, that stupid expression?"

"Yes, yes, I'm familiar?" she says.

"I don't knock on actual wood, because most wood is gross. But I do have to knock on *something* when I have a bad thought. Even if it's just against my leg or whatever."

I stop there. I decide to leave out the beat-off tally and the peeing and the Converse addiction. I think she has plenty to work with.

Dr. S. puts her pen down. "So," she says, "what happens if you *don't* do these things?"

"What do you mean?"

"If you don't wash your hands or check the stove or make a list or knock on wood, what happens?"

"Uh," I stammer, "I don't know. I've never *not* done them."

I think about all the sleepless nights I've spent obsessing over whether the stove was turned off or whether I had to pee again. And then getting up to check the stove and pee again just so I could try to relax.

"Okay, so what happens if, for instance, your hands get dirty and you're not in a place where you can wash them right away?"

I squirm in my seat.

"Well . . . I guess . . . I feel, like, *contaminated*. Like my hands are dirty and then that's gonna get in my mouth or eyes or something and I'm gonna get sick."

I don't know why, but I suddenly feel the urge to prove to Dr. S. that I'm not crazy. I start to get animated. "But here's the thing—I stare at my hands and I can't do anything else until I wash them—even if they're really not that dirty— but I *know I'm not gonna get sick*. Like, I *know* what I'm doing doesn't make any sense."

Dr. S. smiles. "Chuck, the very definition of obsessive-compulsive disorder is having time-consuming, intrusive thoughts and doing repetitive behaviors to reduce anxiety? But just as important, sufferers are *aware* that these thoughts and behaviors are irrational."

Fuck me. Seriously?

"Oh" is all I say.

"Making a clinical diagnosis is not an exact science," she continues, "and will take several sessions. But all signs point toward OCD as you and your parents suspect? In fact, I would go so far as to say your case is, well, *textbook*."

I'm not sure if I'm supposed to be proud of this or what.

"So, uh, now what do we do?" I mumble.

"OCD is linked to abnormalities in the brain, cycles that get caught on repeat. Luckily, there are ways to break the cycles and retrain your brain, so to speak? Have you ever heard of cognitive behavioral therapy, Chuck?"

Even though it's only our second session, I'm already starting to pick up on when Dr. S. is asking an actual question.

"No," I say. "What is it?"

"CBT essentially means exposing you to some of your OCD triggers so that you become desensitized to them?"

"So, like, if I have to turn my lock fourteen times before walking away . . . I just, like, *don't* do that?"

"Gradually, yes. Eventually you will realize that there are no repercussions if you do not perform the task, and that begins to weaken the compulsion in your brain?"

"That sounds . . . hard."

"Many patients find this very difficult, which is why it is a slow process?"

My head is throbbing. I'm beginning to doubt my decision to agree to another session. My senior year is already ruined. The girl I've been waiting for doesn't even know who I am. The last thing I need is this. To be honest, I kinda want to punch Dr. S. right in the face.

"Chuck? Are you listening to me?"

I don't even realize Dr. S. is still talking. I snap out of it and push aside the thought about punching her in the face. But not before I nonchalantly reach down and tap my knee. I hope she doesn't realize I just knocked on wood.

When I sit down in the cafeteria for lunch, Steve and Kanha are already eating. It's the same table we always eat at, of course, and they've reserved my usual seat, lest I freak out.

Kanha is a scrawny Indian kid, and like my not-so-scrawny Indian psychiatrist, he's sometimes hard to understand. Not because he has an accent—he doesn't—but because for some reason he talks like a rapper.

"Yo dog," he says, "Sludgelacker says you're crushing on the new girl."

I play it cool. "Who, Amy?"

"Yeah, Amy. She's sitting right behind you, yo."

I freeze. Is he serious? I spent Calc this morning staring at Amy—she was wearing this cute little bow thing in her hair that still did nothing to tame those bangs—but she's never been in the cafeteria during my lunch period before.

Kanha is laughing at me. Steve is laughing, too, which is kind of annoying because I feel like they're ganging up on me. Very, very slowly I turn around. Holy crap. They're not joking. Amy is sitting at the table behind me, with Stacey and Wendy. I stare for a moment too long and me and Amy's eyes meet for a split second. Shit! I spin back around toward Steve and Kanha, almost spilling my soda in the process.

"She looked at me," I say breathlessly.

"Of course she looked at you, you were staring at her like a psycho," Steve says.

"You're straight trippin' yo," Kanha adds.

"What does that even mean?" I say, starting to get annoyed again.

Kanha is cornered. "Uh, actually I'm not sure," he admits.

"Is Amy already friends with Stacey and Wendy?" I ask. "I mean, if she's in with that crew that means I have no chance. *Shit*." I'm already defeated.

"Chuck," Steve says, waiting for me to look up at him. "Relax. I'm pretty sure Stacey was assigned to show Amy around, you know because she's on student government? And Wendy, well, you know Wendy just follows Stacey wherever she goes. They're probably just being nice or whatever."

"Yeah." I nod. "You're probably right."

Fucking Steve, man. Say what you want about the guy, but he's a great friend. He almost always knows exactly what to say to calm me down.

"Why don't we do this," Steve continues. "Let's see if we can hear what they're talking about."

"That's a good idea, dog," Kanha chimes in.

Me and Steve both just stare at him and roll our eyes. Then all three of us get really quiet and attempt to sorta lean in the direction of Amy's table. It's pretty noisy in the cafeteria but I think I can make out some of what Amy is saying.

"Aw, I think . . . adorable," I hear her say. "Ha ha, that's true. I guess I . . . like that. No, he's cute! Do you . . . when he does . . . antiderivatives."

I look at Steve and Kanha wide-eyed. "*Dude*," I say, "she's talking about Calc! You think, maybe, she's talking about . . . *me*? She definitely said 'antiderivatives.'"

"I thought she said, 'Can't I deliver this,'" Steve says.

"I thought she said, 'Ham and configure tits,'" Kanha says.

"I hate you guys," I retort. "I really think she's talking about me." So what if I'm being a little optimistic? Desperate times call for desperate measures.

Suddenly, Steve and Kanha sit straight up.

"What?" I say.

"Amy," Steve says. "She's getting up."

I don't even have to turn and look because within seconds Amy is standing two feet away from me, about to empty the contents of her lunch tray into the garbage can. She turns and looks back at Stacey and Wendy. She laughs at something they're saying. She has the greatest laugh ever. It's an enthusiastic laugh; she's not holding back—but it's not all high and squeaky. It's perfect.

"I'm telling you," she says to Stacey and Wendy, "I think Mr. Cimaglia is cute. He's like a little pet robot or something."

I feel like I got punched in the stomach. *Chuck, you're a fucking idiot. She wasn't talking about you; she was talking about your stupid Calc teacher!*

Steve and Kanha don't say anything, wisely choosing to let me suffer in silence.

Then, Amy turns back to the garbage can and the crust of her pizza falls off her tray, landing on the floor only inches from my left Con (gray: ambivalent).

Time seems to stand still. *Be a fucking normal human being, Chuck, and pick up the pretty girl's crust.* I try to move my hands but they're frozen. I want to help, but it's just so . . . *gross.* Half-eaten food + school cafeteria floor = no way. I hate myself.

After what seems like an eternity, Amy bends down and picks up the crust. We make eye contact again. My lips start talking before I even realize what's happening.

"Sorry," I mutter in Amy's general direction. *Sorry? Why did you just say that?*

Amy pauses and looks at me the way, I imagine, a scientist would study a mutant monkey he's just captured.

But Amy doesn't seem to judge, or wrinkle her nose at my lack of chivalry or the strange, two-syllable grunt I've just vomited out. Instead, for a brief second, the corner of Amy's mouth turns up. I think she's . . . *grinning* at me. But in a *nice* way.

Before I can completely register what's going on, she stands up, throws her trash away, waves goodbye to Stacey and Wendy, and leaves. It all goes by in a flash.

I look back at Steve and Kanha, who are momentarily speechless.

"Dog," Kanha finally says, "that was weird, yo."

Weird yo indeed.

It's been a rough couple of weeks. In an effort to switch things up, me and Steve hang out at my house for a change, and we dust off the Wii. It's not my system of choice but Beth and her friends like to play it sometimes. I need to blow off some steam and we're not about to go outside, considering it's cold as balls.

The game of the day is Wii Boxing. If you've never played, basically the point is to look like a giant moron. You don't really box so much as you try to pump your fists out in front of you as quickly as possible, kind of like you're doing an invisible elliptical machine in a gym.

Steve's beaten me five times in a row and I'm actually starting to sweat. Luckily (but annoyingly), he gets distracted when Beth meanders into the living room and plants herself on the couch.

"What are you doing?" I half snarl at her.

"Nothing," she says. Then: "You guys suck."

"*You* suck," I say.

She crosses her arms. Steve tries to steal a glance at her

and I take the opportunity to land a savage on-screen uppercut. Still, he comes back and beats me.

"Are you kidding me? How are you so good at this game?"

"Natural talent, Chuck. Natural talent."

"Come on, man, you're like a savant."

"What can I say? Years of practice."

"At what? Jerking off?"

Steve playfully gives me an actual punch on the arm.

"Gross!" Beth interjects from the background.

Me and Steve both stop and look at her.

"Ask her," Steve suggests.

"What? No, dude," I respond.

Steve shakes his head. "Not about me," he whispers. "About *Amy*."

I sigh. As much as I can't stand Beth, and hate the fact that she's so fucking annoying and more popular than me, and has more friends than me, and goes to more parties than me (i.e., more than zero), and has had more boyfriends than I've had girlfriends (again, anything beats zero), Steve has been trying to work into my head that she's a valuable resource.

"Who's Amy?" Beth asks shrilly.

I sigh again. "Just some girl," I say, "who I kinda . . ."

"Who you kinda like!?" Beth exclaims. "Oooooh, Chuck has a girlfriend!"

"Will you shut up? Forget it." *I wish Chuck had a girlfriend . . .*

"Have you talked to her?" Beth asks. I can no longer tell if she's mocking me or not.

I indulge her. "Well, sorta. Once. I didn't pick up her pizza crust and then I said, 'Sorry,' and she sorta smiled at me. I guess you could say that's been the extent."

Beth seems to ignore my entire summary. "Do you know what girls like?" she asks.

I look at Steve, who has clammed shut in the presence of my snot-nosed little sister.

"Soccer players? Rich guys? Confidence?" I offer.

"Not confidence. *Compliments*," she says.

"What?"

"Girls like compliments. Fact. Pick something about her—anything—and say it's pretty."

"Just stroll up to her, pick something, and say it's pretty? That's it?"

"That's it."

I debate this internally.

"Are you fucking with me, Beth?"

"Don't curse at me! I'm telling Mom."

Clearly this conversation has reached its natural conclusion. Beth gets up to leave.

"Hey, Beth," Steve spouts out of nowhere.

Beth pauses and looks around dramatically. "Are you talking to me?" she asks.

What. A. Bitch.

"Yeah," Steve sputters. "Um, I can drive you to school if you want. You know, since I'm already taking Chuck."

Beth looks Steve up and down, perhaps pondering whether he even deserves a verbal response. "No thanks; I have a ride." And then she struts out of the room.

Me and Steve turn back to the Wii.

"I'm gonna pretend that didn't happen," I say.

"Me too," Steve says, as he resumes pummeling me virtually.

I resolve never to play this game with him again.

One, two, three, four, five, six, seven, eight, nine, ten, eleven, twelve, thirteen, fourteen. Wait; that didn't feel right. One, two, three, four, five, six . . . did I miss three? Shit. One more time. One, two, three, four, five, six, seven, eight, nine, ten, eleven, twelve, thirteen, fourteen. Got it.

I've been spinning the lock on my hall locker for the past few minutes. I know it's locked, and there's not even anything that valuable inside, but I'm afraid what might happen if I don't spin it fourteen times and then leave it precisely at zero. Better safe than sorry.

Already mentally drained, I head to Calc. I'm wearing my yellow Cons. Why so nervous? Well, today is the day I'm gonna talk to Amy for the first time (the pizza crust / "sorry" episode notwithstanding). I'm just gonna go up to her, pick something pretty, and compliment her. I mean, this shouldn't be too hard, *everything* about her is pretty. Still, I can't help but wonder in the back of my head if Beth is messing with me. I wouldn't put it past her.

I get to class, nod to Kanha, and notice Amy is already

there, sitting quietly and texting someone. *Who is she texting?* I sit. Her eyes never leave her phone.

As Mr. Cimaglia starts the class, I study Amy's outfit (I'm not worried about her looking back and catching me because she hasn't looked back *once* since I've known her). She's wearing the same shoes she wore the first time I saw her ("ballet flats"—I Googled it). She's got on ripped jeans and a sort of camouflage jacket. But she doesn't look like a tomboy in it, she just looks . . . *hip*. I could never pull off a jacket like that; I'd look like a fucking idiot. But that's it—I can't see what she's wearing underneath the jacket and she's not wearing any jewelry or anything in her hair. I don't have a lot to work with here. I shuffle my Cons beneath my desk.

"Why don't we play a little game," Mr. Cimaglia says to the class. He doesn't put emphasis on any of the words or even ask it like a question (basically the exact opposite of Dr. S.). Unfortunately, Mr. Cimaglia's idea of a "little game" is to quiz us on last night's homework until we get one wrong, then have someone else in the class point out what we screwed up. Socratic method this is not.

"Chuck," Mr. Cimaglia asks, "care to go first?"

I gulp.

"What was your answer to number one?" he demands.

I look at my notebook. Thankfully, I actually did the homework and texted with Kanha to check the answers. I'm reasonably confident.

"B."

"Correct. And number two?"

"C."

"Correct. And number three?"

"A."

"Correct."

I'm on a roll.

"And number four?"

"A again."

"Correct. And number five?" He's such a robot!

"Uh, also A."

"Incorrect."

Damn it. Everyone knows it's never A three times in a row.

Mr. Cimaglia surveys the class. He looks at Amy. "Ms. Huntington, care to share your answer to number five?"

Is this fate? Eh, more likely just a coincidental moment in the painfully insignificant teenage life of one Chuck Taylor.

Amy looks at her notebook. "I got D," she says.

"Correct. Very good. Will you come up to the board and show your work so that Chuck can see what he did wrong?"

Jesus, you don't have to be a dick about it.

Amy walks up to the front of the room. As she slowly copies her work from her notebook onto the board, my mind wanders. How amazing would it be to have Amy as a girlfriend? I imagine us holding hands, going on a picnic, skipping rocks on a pond—apparently I daydream in the 1950s. Of course, in my thoughts I also don't have OCD—I would never touch a dirty rock in real life.

Amy finishes the equation but Mr. Cimaglia is shaking his head. "Unfortunately, Amy," he drones, "it looks like you arrived at the correct answer by accident."

Amy is more self-conscious than embarrassed, but in an

instant I realize both what I did wrong and what she did wrong. Mr. Cimaglia must see the recognition in my eyes because he calls on me and asks me to explain.

"I substituted the wrong variable," I say. "And Amy just accidentally flipped the fraction, which happened to give the right answer anyway. I think."

"That's right," Mr. Cimaglia says. "Good job."

Amy brushes aside her bangs and looks in my direction.

I blurt out, "You're pretty."

Yes, I actually said that. *Out loud.*

Everyone in the class is snickering. Mr. Cimaglia stares at me with a perplexed look. Amy returns to her seat as if nothing happened.

Why on earth did I just do that? Beth said to pick something, not *everything*. And not in front of *everybody*!

The class continues, and mercifully my outburst seems to be quickly forgotten. I thank God for inflicting ADD upon my entire generation. Still, I want to disappear. I turn the page in my notebook and find today's To Do list.

Underneath ~~make bed~~ is: *compliment Amy.*

I cross that off, then add another item underneath: *be a fucking moron.*

I cross that off as well.

Me and Steve are walking to his car after school. I'm once again recounting the play-by-play of how I put the moves on Amy in Calc. He stops dead in his tracks.

"Why would you say that, Chuck?"

"*I don't know.*"

"What were you thinking?"

"*I don't know.*"

"Are you crazy?"

"Probably!"

This time, Steve isn't making me feel any better. We continue walking, but getting scolded by Steve will have to wait because Parker and Ashley Allen are approaching us in the parking lot. Ashley is Parker's buddy on the soccer team, though I've never understood why he isn't on the basketball team considering he's six foot three. (Mental note: he would be perfect for that really tall girl I saw in Dr. S.'s office.)

Parker stops, but since he's standing between us and Steve's car, we're forced to basically approach *him*. I'm still never sure if Parker plays these mind games on purpose. Maybe he's not as dumb as he looks. It's a windy day and his freakin' warm-up pants are flapping around so hard I can see his upper thigh through the opening between snaps.

"What's up, Fudge Packer?" Parker taunts.

I can tell Steve is terrified. "Just leave me alone, Parker."

"What are you gonna do about it?" He nudges Steve in the chest.

I feel like I should say something, anything. But I haven't exactly had much success being on-the-spot today. Plus, I'm kind of a pussy. Thankfully, Ashley intervenes first.

"Come on, Parker, let's get the fuck outta here."

I always kind of liked Ashley. He's the nicest of the asshole jocks, and I almost mean that as a compliment. In a way I envy him. I mean, I assume the only way to survive high school with the name Ashley is to be tough. I wish I was tough.

"Nah, man," Parker says, waving Ashley off, "I want to see what Fudge Packer has to say for himself."

"Screw you, Parker," Steve says. Me, Ashley, Parker, *and* Steve himself are all shocked he just said that.

Uhh!

Parker pushes Steve and Steve falls to the ground, scraping his elbow. Parker stands over him, glowering.

Ashley eyes Principal Rodriguez across the lot. She's not even looking in our direction, but is evidently too close for comfort nonetheless.

"Parker, let's go!"

Parker looks up from Steve and stares me down. He feints like he's gonna push me, too. I flinch. Parker grins. I silently call him Lord Douche. He and Ashley finally stroll away.

I help Steve up. His elbow is bleeding but it's not too bad. His eyes are watery and I think he might cry, but he doesn't. I breathe a sigh of relief; I don't know what I'd do if he started crying.

"You okay?" I ask.

"Yeah, I'm fine. What an asshole."

"Should we tell Mrs. Rodriguez or something?"

"No, it's fine."

I'm not really sure what else to say.

"Let me ask you something," Steve says. "You think Parker is gonna go pro?"

"What, in soccer? Not a chance."

"Exactly. So the way I see it, I've just got to put up with this for a few more months. While we're away at school, he'll drink himself out of whatever meathead university he gets accepted to and end up at West Lake Community College learning transmission repair. And the next time I see Parker, at our ten-year reunion, he'll be working in an auto-body shop and I'll have a hot wife with big-ass fake tits. I can live with that."

"You sure?" I ask.

"Oh yeah. *Huge.*"

Steve doesn't realize I'm talking about him, not his future wife's tits, but I let him have it. He walks off to his car, rubbing his elbow, ever the optimist. I can't help but think he'll reach his breaking point soon, and I better be there to actually help.

"Come on," Steve calls over his shoulder, before adding with a grin, "Have I mentioned how pretty you look today?"

I'm sitting in Dr. S.'s office, continuing our game of cat and mouse. For the past few weeks she's been trying to talk me into trying cognitive behavioral therapy and I've been attempting to argue my way out of it. I think she's starting to get frustrated, and so am I.

"Chuck, I know this is difficult, but the best way for you to overcome your OCD is for you to expose yourself to your triggers, yes?"

"It's not gonna work," I say.

"Then there's nothing to lose. What if we take it very, very slowly? Tomorrow, in between just one of your classes, try *not* to turn your lock fourteen times before walking away. And then just see what happens?"

"But what if my locker isn't locked?"

"Can't you tell it's locked by hearing the click and spinning it once?"

"I guess. But what if it's *not* locked for some reason?"

"Chuck, you've said yourself that there's nothing of real value in there anyway?"

"I know, but . . ."

"And you've also said that you *know* your locker is locked without turning it fourteen times?"

"Yeah, but . . ."

"Chuck, your mind is playing games with you. That's all OCD is, yes? You can't listen to your brain and give in to your compulsions anymore."

"But . . . it *feels good* when I do."

Dr. S. grins. "Exactly."

"Exactly? Exactly what?" I plead.

"Giving in to your compulsions reduces anxiety, which leads to more compulsions, which leads to more anxiety, which leads to your desire to give in to them. It's a vicious cycle? This is *classic* OCD."

Dr. S. always seems unusually excited about how "standard" my case is. I let out a long sigh.

"Chuck, you seem discouraged?"

"It's just that," I mumble, "I thought this would be easier. Like there would be some sort of mind trick or something." God, I sound stupid.

"In a way," she responds, "this *is* a mind trick. There's no need to get frustrated." Dr. S. shifts in her seat and puts her notepad down. "Chuck, if you continue to resist trying CBT, then it is going to be difficult to treat you?"

I don't say anything.

"However, I think we should discuss medication?"

Huh?

"Like, drugs?"

"Have you heard of Lexapro, Chuck?"

"No."

"It's an antidepressant—"

"But I'm not . . ."

Dr. S. raises her hand to stop me as if she's anticipated what I'd say.

"I know you're not depressed, Chuck. But antidepressants like Lexapro are often prescribed to teenagers with OCD symptoms. I've had a lot of success with other patients?"

I can't imagine there's anyone out there like me, who's as *weird* as me.

"Lexapro may help reduce some of your symptoms, hopefully just enough that CBT won't be as difficult to attempt?"

"But I don't wanna get drugged."

How did it come to this? One little Google search, one little Flickapedia article, one harmless conversation with Mom, and next thing I know I'm trapped in a room for fifty minutes a week with a pear-shaped, Nike-wearing shrink who wants to drug me with God knows what. Lexa-who?

"I'm going to write a prescription and speak to your parents. Is that okay?"

"I guess," I mutter. They'll have to force it down my throat.

"Do you want to get better, Chuck?"

"Of course."

"Then let me help you?"

Now *my* eyes are getting watery. This is so stupid. Just let me make my lists and check the stove and I'll be fine. I got by this long. I bury my face in my chest.

"Chuck, are you okay? Would you like a tissue?"

I don't look up.

One, two, three, four, five, six, seven, eight, nine—

"Hey, Chuck."

Someone just said my name. It couldn't be. I refocus on my locker.

One, two, three, four, five, six, seven—

"Chuck?"

I look up. Standing before me . . . is none other than Amy.

"Chuck, right?" she says.

I set the Guinness record for longest stare without blinking.

"Yeah, uh, yes. Hi." It's a start.

"I'm Amy." She pauses. "You know, from Calc?"

I do my very best to pretend that this is not the most important moment of my entire life and that I haven't spent the last month jerking off to her and keeping track of it.

"Oh, hi" is all I can manage.

She extends her hand and I shake it. So soft. I actually might not even wash my palm. For a little while at least.

There's an awkward moment—I'm still not sure what the hell is going on or what I did to deserve this.

"Cool kicks," Amy says.

We both look down at my Cons. They're pink. *Why did I have to be so bored this morning? Idiot!*

"Pink Chucks. Pretty rad."

Wait, I think she seriously likes them.

"Yeah," I say, recovering. "I actually call 'em Cons. You know, to avoid confusion with my name? You know, Chuck / Chucks?" *What the fuck are you babbling about, shut up . . .*

But Amy nods in agreement: "Right on."

I freakin' love her.

"So," she continues, "I was wondering . . . you seem like you really know what you're doing in Cimaglia's class."

"Oh, thanks. Yeah, I kinda like math I guess." *Chuck, why are you making up lies for no reason? You. Are. Retarded.*

"Really?" Amy says. "I can't stand calc. I'm more of a chemistry girl."

Of course, why *wouldn't* she be a chemistry girl? What? My head is spinning.

"So, anyway, I was wondering if maybe you'd be interested in tutoring me for the Calc AP exam. You saw me in class the other day, I have no idea what I'm doing."

This has certainly taken an interesting turn. First thought? Tutoring = quality time. Me likey.

"Yeah, uh, sure. I can do that," I smile.

"Of course I'll pay you and—"

"No, no, no. Definitely not. You don't have to pay me." *Chuck, you're being suave and manly and shit. This is good.*

"Oh I couldn't let you help me and not pay—"

"Absolutely not. I'll tutor you for free. Besides, tutoring

you will probably help me prepare anyway, so that'd be like you paying me to study." I chuckle nervously. *Don't blow it . . .*

"Wow, that's really sweet of you, Chuck."

"No problem, Amy." I realize this is the first time I've ever said her name out loud in front of her—sans the black-board debacle, which I've since stricken from the record. It feels comfortable, like I've been saying it for years.

"So we'll talk soon and figure out a time and a place and everything?" she says.

"That sounds great. Are you gonna be in Calc tomorrow?" I ask.

"Yeah," she smiles quizzically, "why wouldn't I be?"

You're losing it. Get out of this conversation now! Abort!

"I don't know. I was just saying. Well, I'll see you tomorrow then!"

Did I just kinda shout that last line?

"Right on," Amy smiles again. "See you tomorrow."

Honestly, who uses the term "right on"? Only the coolest people on the planet! I can't say "right on"! I'd be labeled a poser immediately!

Amy starts to walk away, then turns back to me.

"Oh, and Happy Valentine's Day."

She smiles, shrugs, then leaves.

Amy Huntington just wished me a motherfucking Happy Valentine's Day. I didn't even know it was Valentine's Day!

I'm not sure what to do with myself. I can't decide what to do first. Do I text Steve to tell him what happened? I'm so flustered. And sweaty. The bell rings. Without thinking, I charge off to my next class. It's a new day.

Only later do I realize I never turned my lock fourteen times.

I'm trying to do homework but I can't get my mind off Amy. I keep replaying our conversation over and over again in my head. It feels good to obsess over something that's, well, good. I'm interrupted mid-daydream.

"Chuck!"

Mom is calling from the kitchen. Honestly, my bedroom and the kitchen are not that far away from each other. There's no need to scream.

I float downstairs. Life is good.

That feeling, though, as always, is fleeting. When I enter the kitchen I can see the serious look on my parents' faces. I immediately do an internal inventory of anything I may have possibly done wrong that I'm about to get grounded for. But everything comes up clean.

"Sit down, Chuck," Dad says.

I do. "What's wrong?" I ask.

"Nothing is wrong," Mom says. "We just want to know how everything is going with Dr. Srinivasan."

Oh.

"It's going fine, I guess." I need to figure out a way to tell them what they want to hear so I don't have to talk about this anymore. Not tonight at least.

"She says that you've kind of . . . hit a wall," Mom says, as I roll my eyes. "You talked to her about taking Lexapro, right?"

"Mom, if you know the answer, why are you asking me?"

Mom realizes she's in delicate territory. "We just want to let you know that we filled the prescription she wrote for you."

Dad takes an orange pill bottle out of a small paper bag and unceremoniously places it on the kitchen table in front of me.

"It's covered by insurance," he states proudly.

Dad. Never ceases to amaze me.

"We also want to let you know," Mom continues, "that we're not going to make you take it, but we think you should consider it."

"Well, I'm not gonna."

"Chuck—"

"I don't need pills. I'm not depressed."

"No one said you're depressed, Chuck," Mom says. "Lots and lots of people take medication like this. Millions of people in fact."

I take a big, obnoxious breath.

Dad picks up the bottle and hands it to me, forcing me to hold it.

"Just think about it," he says.

I stare at the bottle. There it is in black and white:

PLAINVILLE PHARMACY
DR. SRINIVASAN, AHLADITA

TAYLOR, CHARLES
TAKE ONE TABLET DAILY
LEXAPRO

And my day had been going so well . . .

After another twenty minutes of idle chatter with Mom and Dad, I trudge back to my room. I sit at my desk, staring at the bottle of pills again. Then I open the drawer closest to my bed. Ironically, this is where I keep my masturbation tally (for easy reaching). I throw the Lexapros into the drawer and shut it. Case closed.

I slump into my desk chair. Then I hear a *ping* from my laptop. It's a new email. Probably Steve sending me some awful YouTube clip. I check my messages. It's not at all what I expect:

> **Amy Huntington wants to be friends with**
> **you on Facebook.**

Then there's a little thumbnail picture of Amy, flashing a peace sign and winking. Amazing.

I've never accepted a friend request faster in my life. Granted I don't get many, but still, I'm all over it.

Like two seconds later, I get a Facebook message from Amy. Honestly, my young heart can't take this much drama in one day. I open the shit out of the message. Amy wants to know if we can meet on Thursday after school at the library to start studying. I debate whether I should wait to write back so I don't come off too eager, but decide I'm already playing with house money. I type that Thursday works for me. I can't figure out how to end my message, though. I write:

Peace,
Chuck

Then I realize that I'm *not fucking cool enough* to sign messages with "Peace." I just go with:

—Chuck

Simple, yet elegant. I hold my breath and hit Reply.

Rocking tan Cons today: anxious. I'm sitting in the school library, waiting to meet Amy. It's all I've thought about all day—every day in fact since she Facebooked me. The time has come. She's here.

Amy sits down at the overly large table I've commandeered for our study session. She's wearing the camouflage jacket again. "Hey, you," she says.

If it was socially acceptable to swoon, I would.

"Hey," I say, playing it cool.

"How crazy was that today in Cimaglia?" she says.

This morning in Calc, Kanha got food poisoning or something and barfed all over his desk in the middle of class. Just from the sight of it, Wendy started to feel sick, too, and ran out of the room. I feel bad (more so for Kanha than for Wendy), but my stomach was sore from laughing. Good times.

"Yeah, that was awesome," I say. "Well, not awesome. But, you know . . . crazy."

Amy just smiles. She puts me at ease. She's kind of like Steve, but with a vagina.

She starts to get her books out.

I blurt out, "I like your jacket." I've begun to realize that I'm much better at paying compliments when I don't think about them so much ahead of time. That wasn't so hard.

"Really? Thanks," Amy says. "It's really, really old. From before I was born. It was my dad's and it shrank so much that he just gave it to me. And now it like totally fits. Weird how that works, huh?"

"So weird," I say. *Stupid.* "The camouflage is cool." *Okay, decent recovery.*

"Thanks. Yeah, my dad was in the army. This was like his first jacket. That's actually why I move around so much."

"Because of the jacket?"

Amy laughs. "No, because my dad was in the army."

Amy thinks I'm making a joke when I'm actually just making a fool of myself. I'm officially entering foreign territory. And I like it.

"Every time he got transferred to a new base, we all had to move. This is my third high school. And hopefully my last, considering we graduate this year. Fingers crossed."

"That's pretty crazy that you move around so much. I don't know if I could handle that," I say.

"Well, there are some good things about it. I've gotten to meet a lot of chill people, and see the whole country. I kind of like the idea of not *being* from one specific place, you know?"

"I hate being from Plainville."

"I think it's nice. It's quaint. Better than a lot of the other places I've been. I like the vibe here. There's good energy."

I really don't know how to even respond to that, so I don't.

"My dad's doing a consulting project nearby, that's why we moved. He's not in the army anymore so I think we'll be here for a while."

Best news I've heard all decade.

"Do you have any brothers or sisters?" I ask. I envision an older brother. A marine. Angry. At me.

"Nope. It's just me, my mom, my dad, and Buttercup."

"Buttercup?"

"My dog. She's a puggle."

"A what?"

"A puggle. Part beagle, part pug."

"Oh, I didn't know that was a thing."

"She's my best friend in the whole world. My mom takes care of her when I'm at school. I'm always texting her to make sure she walks her and changes her water and all that stuff."

"That's cool," I manage. Dogs: not my thing.

"Thanks again for helping me with calc," Amy says. "I really appreciate it. And I promise to pay you back some-how when I rock the AP exam!" She touches my arm as she says this and I feel slightly light-headed.

Amy opens up her books and I do the same. She looks at me and smiles. I smile back involuntarily. We just stare at each other.

"So," Amy says finally, "where should we start?"

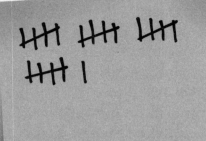

S o?"
    "So, what?"

I'm in my room, talking to Steve on the phone and being coy because today was the greatest day ever and I've always wanted to try to be coy.

"How was the study session?" Steve asks excitedly.

"Pretty good. She's a little weak in antiderivatives so we spent a lot of time on that."

"Chuck, I'm gonna fucking kill you. I don't give a shit about calc. How was *Amy*?"

Being coy is making Steve angry. I smirk to myself: this is fun. Then I give it a rest.

"It was awesome, man," I say. "She's so cool. It's a little intimidating, but not really because she's so cool. We only spent about twenty minutes studying, the rest of the time we just talked."

"About what?"

"About everything. About how she moves around a lot.

About how she always wanted to be in a band but she can't sing or play an instrument."

"That would make being in a band pretty difficult."

"I know; that's what I said!" I shake my head, amazed at Amy's boundless aspirations. "She also told me," I continue, "that Stacey and Wendy are 'nice.' I don't think she's, like, good friends with them or anything, which is probably good for me. Oh, and she definitely doesn't have a boyfriend, thank God."

"You asked her that?"

"No way. She mentioned that she had some ex-boyfriend in San Diego and he was a real asshole. Since she moves around a lot she doesn't like to get 'too attached,' whatever that means."

"Well, that's not good," Steve says. "If she doesn't like to get attached, doesn't that mean she doesn't want a new boyfriend?"

Girls. Who knows *what* they mean?

"Well," I say, "there were some good signs. She touched my arm. I once read in one of Beth's stupid magazines that girls do that when they're interested."

"What magazine?"

"I don't know; I think it was—wait, why do you care what magazine? Steve, don't be a douche and get a subscription to a girly magazine just because Beth reads it and you're trying to learn more about her."

"What makes you think I'm gonna do that?"

Now who's playing coy?

"Anyway," I say, trying not to think about Steve and my sister, "she also said that I'm really funny."

"What?"

"Yeah, she thinks I'm funny."

"Dude," Steve says, "you're definitely going to Bangtown."

"Bangtown?"

"Yeah, you know, the place where people go when they have sex? Get it?"

"She's not having sex with me," I say, my head flooded with thoughts of Amy having sex with me.

"Why not?" Steve says. "The number one thing that girls are looking for in a guy is a sense of humor. That's like a scientifically proven fact."

"Really?"

I sit up in bed and look at myself in the mirror across the room. My hair does nothing. It just kind of 'fros up. Putting gel in it only makes it worse. I've got big ears. Not Dumbo big, but big enough to grab on to. I have no cheekbones or any facial definition to speak of. I suck. No one wants to go to Bangtown with this.

"Chuck?"

"Yeah."

"Are you staring at your cheekbones in the mirror?"

I lie back down.

"Maybe."

"Chuck, you got this. The APs aren't for like two and a half months. That's a lot of time. She just moved to town, she doesn't really know anyone, she doesn't even know what a dork you are. You're all she's got."

Wait a minute, that's kind of offensive. Then I realize it's true.

"Okay," I concede.

"When's your next study session?"

"Wednesday."

"Are we still going to the movies after school on Tuesday?"

"Yeah, but my mom thinks we should leave fifteen minutes earlier."

"I'm sure she does. What are you gonna do now?"

"I don't know; nothing."

"All right, I'll see you in school."

"Later, Steve."

I hang up. I think of Amy. Time to make a tally.

Pretty tired today: orange Cons. A flu bug has been going around so the school has installed a bunch of automatic hand sanitizer dispensers throughout the building. I *love* hand sanitizer. I think I'm the only student who uses it. I guess some OCD trumps other OCD because I've altered my usual route from English to European History to take advantage of the dispenser stationed near the gym. It feels so good when it hits my skin. It's like a rush directly to my brain. I want to bathe in this shit.

"What are *you* doing in this hallway?"

I look up and see Steve approaching.

"Ah, hand sanitizer. I should have known. Let me get some of that." He sticks his hand under the sensor and gets a squirt, perhaps in an attempt to make me feel less weird. "What's going on?"

"I have Euro now," I say. "The homework was so—" I stop.

Amy is walking in our direction. Never changing my route through school means I'm not used to seeing people unexpectedly. It raises my anxiety level. More so because it's Amy, of course.

She walks up to us. "Hey, Chuck!" It's weird because I still feel like I'm surprised every time she knows who I am.

"Hey, Amy."

She smiles, I of course smile, and Steve is left standing there like an idiot.

"I'm Steve," he says, giving me a dirty look.

"Oh, sorry," I say sheepishly.

"Great to meet you, Steve," Amy says. "Chuck talks about you a lot."

"Well, I wouldn't say *a lot*," I interject.

"How's the studying going?" Steve asks. I try to remember the last time I even saw him talk to a girl besides my stupid sister.

"So far so good," Amy says. "Actually, Chuck, I was about to text you. You think we could study after school today instead of tomorrow? I have some family thing I gotta do tomorrow that I totally spaced on."

Oh, Amy Huntington, don't you realize you could literally ask me anything and I would say yes?

"Yeah, that's cool," I say. "I'm free today."

"Right on," Amy says. "I'll see you later. It was nice to meet you, Steve."

"You too," Steve murmurs.

Amy trots off, all Amy-like and cool.

Steve waits until she's out of earshot.

"What the fuck, Chuck?"

"What?" I say.

"I thought we were going to the movies today."

I'd like to say it was a mistake and I had forgotten all

about my plans with Steve, but that would be a lie.

"Oh, I totally forgot."

"Chuck, you're the worst liar ever."

"I'm sorry. It's *Amy*. What was I supposed to do?"

Steve sighs, shakes his head, and walks off.

I can honestly say I have no regrets.

Me and Amy are at our usual table. I mean, this is only our second time hanging out, er, studying, but I have internally designated it as "our" table.

"You want some?" Amy is eating a granola bar. One of those "stiff" ones that crumble into a billion pieces as soon as you take a bite.

"I'm good," I say. Amy happily munches away. I can't for the life of me comprehend how people can just eat food with their hands and not wash them immediately afterwards. The crumbs on our usual table are bugging me. I'm hankering for some sanitizer. I promise myself I will never, ever tell Amy about my OCD.

"Hey what's the deal with this Senior Weekend thing?" Amy asks. "People are freaking out about it."

"It's pretty stupid," I say. "Everyone is just gonna go to some field and drink. People are probably gonna be puking all over the place."

"I think it sounds fun. I mean, not the puking part. I like camping."

Why does everyone like camping so much? It's like being voluntarily homeless!

"Yeah, I guess," I say. "I'm probably not gonna go."

"Really? Aww, you should go. It won't kill you."

When Amy says it, it almost seems true. Almost.

"Soooo," Amy purrs, changing the subject, "what was with that comment you made a few weeks ago in Calc?"

"Huh?"

"Cimaglia made me stand up in front of the class and you just blurt out, 'You're pretty'?"

Oh my God. I want to hide. Face. Getting. Red.

"Uh, umm, uh, well, uh . . ." I'm literally stuttering. "Sorry about that."

I wish someone would shoot me in the face. I knock on wood / my knee.

"It's totally fine," Amy says. "Just kinda random for math class is all."

"I say it a lot," I stammer. *What?*

"You go around telling girls they're pretty a lot?"

"Yeah. I mean, uh, yeah. All the time."

"Oh," she says, "and here I thought I was the only one." She feigns a frown.

Is what I'm thinking is happening actually happening? Is Amy Huntington sorta kinda maybe . . . flirting with me?

"No," I blather, "that's not what I meant. I've actually never said that to anyone before. I'm sorry."

"No need to apologize. I thought it was nice."

"You did?"

"Sure. What girl doesn't like a compliment?"

Mental note: listen to Beth more often but never admit it.

"Anywho," Amy says, "I was just always wondering where that came from, and now that we're friends I thought it would be okay to ask you. NBD."

She looks down at her calc textbook.

I hang on her words. I can't decide if being Amy's friend is a breakthrough or a death sentence.

She doesn't say anything, or even look at me any differently, but I can just sense that Dr. S. hates me. After almost two months of head shrinking, we still haven't made any progress. I'm too stubborn/scared to try any therapy, and the Lexapros are gathering dust in my room (this is just an expression of course; my room is spotless). In a tactic I assume is meant to lull me into a false sense of security, Dr. S. has begun asking me more benign, personal questions as opposed to hammering me about my symptoms.

"How's your love life, Chuck?"

It's amazing to me how adults are able to take awkward situations and make them even awkwarder. But I'm feeling pretty frustrated today (white Cons) and I figure I can use all the help I can get, so I take the bait.

"There's actually a girl I've been hanging out with. Amy."

Dr. S. peers at me from behind her glasses. I feel like she

doesn't believe me and is adding *delusional nutcase* to my diagnosis.

"Amy? That's a pretty name."

Yes, Doc, it is.

"We've been hanging out a lot. I've actually been helping her, well, tutoring her, in calc."

"But you hate math, yes? You must really like this girl?"

True on both accounts.

"I guess. But we're just friends." Amy said so herself.

"But you'd like to be more than just friends?"

"I mean, yeah."

"Chuck, how do you think your obsessions and compulsions are affecting your relationship, or lack thereof, with Amy?"

Huh, that was a much more abrupt transition than I expected. Dr. S. is slipping. I'll play along.

"Well, it doesn't help. Sometimes her backpack is covered in dog hair. It kind of makes me a little nauseous. She's so pretty—and clean. Very clean. But the dog hair—it's not good."

"Why don't you try touching the dog hair?"

"What?"

"We've talked about what's called 'habituation' before, yes? If you can expose yourself to one of your triggers, and refrain from performing your compulsion, that will help you habituate—or get used to it—and reduce your anxiety."

I merely shake my head. No.

"Chuck, one dog hair can't hurt you, right?"

"What do you mean?"

"If a strand of dog hair got on your arm right now, would it be harmful?"

"It would be disgusting. But no, I guess not."

"So try taking one little, tiny dog hair off of Amy's backpack and putting it on your arm, and see what happens?"

"Nothing is gonna happen."

"You're right, nothing *is* going to happen. That's the point, see?"

"This is stupid."

Dr. S. puts her pen down. But she definitely puts it down with a little extra emphasis. That was a "fuck you" pen putdown.

"Have you given any more thought to taking the Lexapro?"

"I thought you weren't gonna ask me about that anymore?"

"I feel like we are reaching a critical stage in your care, Chuck. How are you going to maintain normal relationships when you get older, not just with girls but with your friends and family, if you don't try to beat this thing?"

"Maybe it will go away on its own. My mom said that she had some symptoms when she was a kid that eventually went away."

Dr. S. ignores this wishful thinking. "Chuck, the Lexapro I've prescribed is a very low dosage. I'll be monitoring you closely. I think you'll find it helps?"

I don't say anything.

"Wouldn't Amy want you to get better?"

I do not like this. I do not like Dr. S.'s tone. I do not like her saying Amy's name. I do not like her playing the Amy card.

"Amy has no idea there's anything wrong with me. And I plan on keeping it that way."

"Don't you think, Chuck, that she's going to find out eventually?"

I sure hope not.

Sloppy Joes in the cafeteria today so obviously I've brought lunch from home. Since she just showed up out of nowhere in January, Amy keeps having to switch up her schedule so she can fit in everything she needs to graduate. She was only in my lunch period that one fateful day before she ended up dropping it and taking an extra class instead. So for now at least, it's just me, Steve, and Kanha.

"Yo, dogs," Kanha says. "The Barrys want to know if we wanna join Mathletes. A few spots opened up."

Barry and Barry (no relation) are two uber-dorks in Calc BC and the co-captains of the PWLJFKHS Mathletes squad. So clearly they get all the chicks.

"Are you serious, Kanha?" I say. "Why would we want to do that? You know I hate math."

"Then why are you spending like every day after school doing extra calc work, homie?" he responds.

"Because," Steve interjects abruptly, "whatever Amy wants, Amy gets."

"What's that supposed to mean?" I say.

"You know what it means."

Since I started tutoring Amy a couple of weeks ago, things between me and Steve have gotten a little weird. Blowing him off that time when we were supposed to go to the movies was just the beginning. While I haven't broken any plans with him since, I haven't exactly gone out of my way to *make* plans with him either. Amy keeps wanting to study after school and I just can't bring myself to say no. Quite frankly, I don't *want* to say no.

"Whoa, whoa, whoa," Kanha says, putting down a french fry. "Do you guys have beef?" It's really hard to take Kanha seriously when he talks like that.

"No, there's no 'beef,'" Steve says diplomatically. "Chuck has just had more important things to do than hang out with me."

Huh, on second thought that wasn't very diplomatic at all.

"Come on, Steve," I say, "gimme a break. Don't be pissed off. It's Amy."

"That's all you ever say: 'It's Amy.'"

"Well, it is. She's my friend."

"I'm not pissed off, Chuck. I'm just worried about you."

"What are you worried about?"

"You promise you're not gonna get mad?"

"I'm not gonna get mad, Steve. What are you worried about?"

"Well, what if Amy *isn't* your friend?"

"What do you mean?"

"I mean, what if she's just, like, hanging out with you because you're tutoring her for free?"

The thought had definitely crossed my mind. The new, hot girl flirting with the geeky weirdo just enough to get him to do what she wants is not a hard storyline to imagine. But Amy would never do that.

"Fuck you, Steve," I say. "I'm not that dumb. Don't be jealous."

"Oh, snap!" Kanha says.

Steve immediately backtracks. "I didn't mean it like that, Chuck. I shouldn't have said anything. I just don't want her to end up fucking you over."

"She won't," I say. "I know what I'm doing." I decide to offer an olive branch. "Wii Boxing at my house after school?"

"I don't know," Steve smirks, "I'm thinking about joining Mathletes."

"For reals?" Kanha says, lighting up.

"No, you idiot," Steve says to Kanha. "I'm kidding. Why do you want to join Mathletes?"

"There's still a couple of competitions left in the year and you get to meet honeys from other schools, yo!"

"What Kanha is saying," I tell Steve, "is that he wants to join Mathletes for the women. Quite possibly the dumbest idea in human history."

Steve laughs. I think our little tiff is over. When all else fails, gang up on the Indian kid who talks like Jay-Z.

"Hey," Kanha says, getting defensive, "we don't all have bangin' ladies to tutor like you, Chuck. I'm trying to expand my horizons, dog."

"Well can you expand your horizons somewhere else?" Steve says. "Stacey Simpson is sitting behind you and is wearing kind of a see-through top. You're blocking my view of her cannons."

Kanha ducks down. Me and Steve share a laugh—and a peek.

HH HH HH
HH HH

A my chuckles. "You can't sit still today."

She's right. I'm fidgeting in my seat at our usual table in the library. I've been feeling restless and antsy all day. Antsy = purple Cons. I can't remember the last time I wore them.

"I know," I say. "I don't know why."

"I do," Amy says. "You have spring fever."

"What?"

"It's March; it's the first nice day of the year. We need to get outside."

"But we have a lot to get through today."

"You're only young once, right? I think we'll live without studying for one day."

"Okay. What do you want to do?"

"Why don't you walk me home?" Amy grins.

The new, hot girl flirting with the geeky weirdo just enough to get him to do what she wants would never blow off studying just to have the weirdo walk her home. I don't know what Steve is talking about.

"Okay," I say, careful to hold back my glee. "Let's go."

It's the most spontaneous thing I've ever done, ever. Hey, baby steps.

Amy lives right on the border between Plainville and West Lake. It'll be a little bit of a hike for me to walk home after I drop her off, but, you know, who gives a shit? You're only young once, right?

We stroll home, chatting. It's unusually warm out. Life actually feels pretty damn good right now.

"So Stacey and Wendy asked me to serve on the prom committee," Amy says.

"Oh yeah?"

"I'm not gonna do it, though. I have to squeeze in all these classes, and prom is kinda lame."

"How come you think prom is lame but Senior Weekend is cool?"

"I don't know. It's kind of sweet that it's a tradition that's passed down by the kids, you know? It's *our* thing. Prom is just so, like, *corporate*."

I have never nor will ever use the term "corporate" to describe something that's lame. Amy has once again demonstrated her dominance over me in the cool department.

"Chuck, I just want to say thank you again for helping me with calc. It's been fun hanging." She smiles that amazing smile.

It takes all my energy to remain upright. I manage to squeak out, "No problem."

"Well, we're here."

We stop in front of Amy's house. I'm just grateful we've

stopped walking because Amy's compliment has made me woozy.

"Huh," I say as we walk through the gate in a fence that surrounds her front yard, "this looks exactly like my house." Was every fucking house in Plainville built by the same architect?

I hear a bark, then the doggy door on Amy's front door swings open and out bounds her dog. He's a little bigger than I expected, golden yellow, and enthusiastic as hell. He runs into Amy's arms and she scoops him up.

"Hey, girl! I missed you so much," Amy says.

I keep forgetting it's a *she*, not a *he*. Like I said, dogs: not my thing.

"I want you to meet someone," Amy says to the dog. "Chuck, this is Buttercup. Buttercup, this is Chuck."

She takes Buttercup's paw and extends it toward me. *She actually wants me to shake her dog's hand?* I try not to visibly grimace as I comply. Her paw isn't as gross as I think it'll be, but I can feel the dog's smell being transferred to my fingers. I shudder but Amy doesn't notice. She puts Buttercup down and the dog starts running in circles around us, occasionally stopping to sniff my Cons or jump up at my crotch. This is not good.

"I've lived in so many cities and gone to so many schools," Amy says, "but I've always been able to count on Buttercup. She's like my only constant, you know?"

"Totally," I say. I don't get it. It's a fucking dog.

Amy kneels down and starts rubbing Buttercup's neck and ears. "I know it's silly," she says, "but she really is my best friend. I don't know what I'd do without her." Amy looks up at me, standing there like a moron and trying to hold my breath. "You can pet her."

I gulp. "No, that's okay."

"Come on, Chuck," Amy says playfully. She takes my hand—which feels awesome—and places it on the back of Buttercup's neck—which feels awful. I pet Buttercup, and I guess she likes it because she sticks her tongue out and starts panting. The dog smell is getting stronger and Buttercup is starting to shed on my jeans. My anxiety level shoots through the roof. I feel like I might freak out at any second. Amy is in another world, totally lost in her stupid dog. I can't let her see me like this.

"I think I'm gonna head home," I manage. "It's gonna get dark soon."

I feel hives start to form on the back of my neck but know there's nothing actually there.

"Okay," Amy says, standing. "Thanks for walking me home." She gives me a hug and I'm almost too preoccupied to fully appreciate it. Over Amy's shoulder, I can see Buttercup just staring up at me and panting. Is she taunting me?

"I'll see you tomorrow," Amy says, smiling.

"You too," I respond, and then dart off in the wrong direction.

I finally get my bearings and jog home. I walk in, toss all my clothes in the hamper, and jump in the shower. I take a long shower, long enough for the smell to disappear and to make sure there's not a single dog hair on me.

My heartbeat finally returns to normal, but when I close my eyes I can still hear Buttercup barking.

"Senior Weekend is less than three months away. People are starting to make plans."

I'm loitering at Steve's locker after school, attempting to make more of an effort to hang out with him.

"So?" I respond.

"So, have you thought any more about, I don't know, going on the trip we've been talking about forever?"

"I told you this already, Steve, it's not my thing."

"You know, I have a little OCD, too. I always check over my homework like ten times before I hand it in. And I always have to make sure I land on an even price when I'm filling up my car with gas."

Of all my pet peeves, this could be number one: when people say, "I have a little OCD, too." Just because you flick your light switch a couple of times or are really anal about organizing your garage does not make you OCD. Everyone has a couple of weird things like that. Saying "I have a little OCD, too" makes it seem like I'm a drama queen or something. I spent close to two hours last night getting in and out of bed to check the fucking stove and then go pee. That's the real deal.

"Whatever, man," I say. "It's not the same."

"I just don't want you to miss out and then regret it, Chuck. I mean, what does Amy think?"

So now Steve also thinks it's appropriate to play the Amy card.

"I don't know. I guess she's gonna go."

"And don't you want to be on an overnight trip where she's gonna be?"

That's not a bad point, but the Amy card really gets me riled up faster than it should.

"You just want me to go because otherwise *you* won't go," I say.

"Hey, don't get mad at me just because you're too messed up in the head to go on a little trip," Steve says.

I just look at him incredulously.

"I *can* go without you, Chuck," he continues. "I can go with Kanha."

I hadn't really considered that. I guess things with Steve are still rockier than I thought. I'm about to try to smooth things over when Parker, everyone's favorite soccer player, turns the corner.

"Oh shit," I mutter.

"What?" Steve turns around and spots Parker as well, but it's too late to flee. Within moments, he's upon us.

"Gimme five bucks, Fudge Packer."

"What? No."

"I said, give me five bucks."

"I don't have any money on me. Leave me alone."

Parker raises his fist and Steve flinches. I flinch a little, too. None of the stragglers in the hallway even notice what's happening. I quickly reach into my pocket and pull out a crumpled five-dollar bill, forgetting for the moment that I can't stand touching money.

"Here," I say to Parker. "Take it."

Parker sizes me up, then takes the bill. Then he throws it on the floor at Steve's feet.

"Pick it up, Fudge Packer."

Okay, I didn't see *this* coming. It's like Parker *practices* bullying techniques in his spare time. Steve doesn't say anything.

"I said, *pick it up*."

Seeing this as yet another battle he can't win, Steve meekly bends down, picks up the money, and hands it to Parker, who grins like the Lord Douche he is.

"Pussy," Parker scowls. Then he walks away, exits the building, and heads toward the parking lot.

"Thanks, man," Steve says to me after a moment. "I guess I owe you five bucks."

"Don't worry about it," I say, knowing I'll probably add it to a To Do list anyway.

Steve doesn't look so good. He's pretty shaken. I sense there's not much more of this he can take.

"Hey," I say, desperately trying to think of anything at all to cheer him up, "if you want, maybe I could put in a good word for you with Beth." *Wait, why did you promise that of all things?*

Steve's eyes light up. I have a feeling that if Steve could

go back in time, he would still risk getting his ass kicked by Parker if it meant he'd get the chance with Beth I've just offered.

"Really?" he says.

"Sure," I say hesitantly, "but I'm telling you she doesn't listen to me."

"Gotta start somewhere, right? Thanks, Chuck!"

Steve goes to pack up his backpack. I don't think I've ever seen quite such a swing of emotions in such a short time. But then I look through the window behind Steve, spot someone getting into Parker's truck with him, and everything changes.

What the fuck? It's Beth.

When I get home from school, Beth is the only one in the house. She's holed up in her room but I can hear music blasting through the door. My guess is she's on the phone and Facebook simultaneously, having inane conversations with dozens of friends. I knock and then walk in. My assumption is correct.

Beth swivels around in her desk chair like the bad guy in a movie, sees me, and sneers.

"I'll call you back in five seconds, okay?" she says to whoever is on the phone. Apparently that's how much of her precious time I'm worth.

She lowers the music. "What do *you* want?"

"I'm just curious how you get to and from school," I say.

Steve likes to grab coffee in the morning so he always gets me a few minutes early, before Beth leaves. And I almost always get home after her. I just assumed she was taking the bus after spurning all of Steve's offers for a ride.

"None of your business," Beth says.

"Well, it is my business if I tell Mom and Dad that you're getting a ride from someone they don't even know."

Beth sighs. "Parker Goldberg takes me."

"Since when?"

"I don't know, for a while. I met him at a party at the beginning of the year. Who cares?"

Beth was at a party? I guess my invitation got lost in the mail.

"I care. Parker is, like, the biggest douche bag ever."

"No he's not. I think he's nice."

Nice?

"He's much cooler than you," she adds.

"Beth, Parker has been picking on Steve for like nine years."

Beth rolls her eyes. "So? What do you want me to do about it?"

"Don't you kind of feel bad about that?"

"No, I feel like I want a ride to school with the captain of the soccer team."

You gotta hand it to her—at least she's honest.

"Why don't you just come with me and Steve?"

"Steve's car is gross and I don't want to ride to school with *you*."

"I don't see what the big deal is."

I can see a multitude of Facebook notifications piling up on Beth's computer screen. I'm unlikely to have her attention much longer.

"Chuck, I'm a little busy. Are you gonna tell Mom and Dad on me or what? They think I'm taking the bus. Don't be a tattletale."

I really don't have the energy to deal with this anymore. I have enough problems.

"No, I won't tell on you."

"Thanks."

"It's just that . . ."

Beth groans. "*What?*"

"Well," I say, "Steve kinda . . . Steve thinks . . . Steve has been saying . . ."

"Will you spit it out already?"

I decide this is not the time or the place, and that there may never be a time or place.

"Nothing. Forget it."

Beth dismisses me and turns back to her computer.

I sheepishly make my way out of her room.

Beth calls out: "What happened with that girl?"

I turn around. "What?"

"What happened with that girl you were talking about? Amy."

I'm suspicious whenever Beth takes any interest at all in my personal life.

"Why do you care?"

"I want to know if you took my advice and gave her a compliment."

"Yeah," I say. "It didn't work."

"You probably did it wrong."

"Whatever," I mutter, and leave.

I head downstairs to the kitchen and perform my stove ritual. I place the palm of my right hand on each burner to make sure it's cold, and go around in a clockwise direction. Then I stare at each knob, making sure all of them are turned exactly to Off. Then I stare for a while at the indicator light that glows when a burner is on, making sure it's definitely off and not malfunctioning. During all this, I contemplate what or what not to tell Steve about my conversation with Beth.

I start my stove ritual over again, just in case.

Forty-five minutes into our study session and me and Amy haven't even opened our books yet. In the past month, we've hung out a few times a week, but studying calc is increasingly being pushed aside in favor of, well, hanging out. I'm not complaining, though, and that's not just because I hate math.

"Do you want to get married one day?" Amy asks.

One of Amy's favorite pastimes, it seems, is asking me hypothetical questions to see how I'll react. She almost always laughs at what I respond, sometimes I think even *with* me instead of *at* me. I'm feeling more and more comfortable around her—the most comfortable I've ever felt with a girl.

"Yes, I want to get married one day," I say.

"Do you want to have kids?"

"Sure."

"How many?"

"2.5."

Amy bursts out laughing. "2.5? How can you have 2.5 kids?"

"The average family has 2.5 kids. I read that somewhere."

"But you can't have half a kid!"

"I know; that's just the average."

Amy laughs again. As much as I adore her smile, her laugh is music to my ears—like audible hand sanitizer.

"Who wants to be average?" she says.

That's one thing of many that worry me about me and Amy's relationship (or, as Dr. S. would say, lack thereof). Amy seems to be operating on a completely different level than me. Amy wouldn't dream of being average. She's lived all around the country, she rocks her dad's sweet old army jacket, she wants to be in a band, she says things like "right on" and "corporate." She's out there. Meanwhile, I'd kill to be average. Average is my *goal*. But of course I could never share that with her.

"Have you ever been in love?" she asks.

I briefly consider answering "Yes," hoping she thinks I'm talking about her. But that seems lame and/or I chicken out.

"No," I say. "What about you?"

I imagine Amy has had plenty of opportunities to be in love.

"Me neither," she says, surprisingly.

"Really?"

"At least I don't think I have," she adds. "I figure I would know it when I see it."

"Yeah, probably," I say, having no idea.

"Let's try something easier," Amy says. "Have you ever made out in the backseat of a car?"

My body temperature rises instantly. Every once in a while, Amy will throw out a question like that—a question about hooking up—and it makes my insides spasm. That's not the kind of question you ask your tutor, or even your platonic guy friend. At least I don't think it is, never having been either myself before this.

"No," I reply, "I've never made out in the backseat of a car. But I also don't have a car."

Amy bursts out laughing once again. "What does that have to do with anything?"

"Well how can you make out in the backseat of a car if you don't have one?"

"Chuck, it could be someone else's car."

"Oh, yeah. I guess."

This is painful to admit, but sitting here, with Amy, in the library, talking about making out . . . well, I get a hard-on. It just happens. Amy + the thought of making out = boner. Even though it's well hidden under the table, I'm terrified she's going to somehow find out.

"Are you okay, Chuck?" Amy asks. "You look a little pale."

That's because the blood from my face is rushing to my dick.

"Yup, I'm fine," I grimace.

The one thing I want in life more than anything is to be with Amy, romantically. We're friends, we talk about everything (well, besides my OCD), we see each other all the time, but it's just not happening. That's why I'm wearing my white Cons again today: so fucking frustrated.

"Stand up," Amy says. "I want to see who's taller. Let's go back to back."

I glance at my crotch. I won't be standing any time soon.

Dad is dropping me off for another worthless session with Dr. S. because he needs to run some errands. It's annoying because it seems like my appointments are on different days every week, depending on who needs which car. Dad is listening to a basketball game on the radio. I can't follow it for the life of me.

"How's school?" he asks.

"Fine."

Conversation is sparse. But I don't think it's because we have nothing to say to each other; I think Dad just wants to listen to the game.

"Mom says you've been tutoring a girl?"

Mom had forced it out of me during one of her trademark interrogation sessions.

"Yeah," I say, "my friend Amy."

"How much is she paying you?"

"She's not."

"Why not?" Dad looks at me, unable to hide the accountant within.

"I don't know, Dad, it just doesn't seem right."

"Least you could do is chip in for some of these therapy sessions. There's a co-pay, you know."

I have no idea what a co-pay is and I think he's kidding, but I also know that Dad has been skeptical about this process from the beginning. I'm not sure he thinks OCD is a real thing.

"Very funny," I say. "But I can't charge her."

"You like this girl or something?"

I take offense at the way he says this. So what if I do like this girl? Is that so hard to believe?

"I dunno. Maybe," I say.

Dad nods his head in a kind of "I both understand and am impressed" sort of way. He reaches over and turns the game down ever so slightly.

"What's her name again?"

"Amy."

"Have you asked her out?"

I roll my eyes. "Dad, people don't just, like, ask people out anymore."

"They don't?" he says coyly. "Then what do they do?"

Good question. I don't know what they do.

"She probably doesn't even like me like that anyway."

"Have you told her how you feel?"

"No."

"Well, you miss a hundred percent of the shots you don't take."

"What?"

"You miss a hundred percent of the shots you don't take. Wayne Gretzky said that. He's a hockey play—"

"I know who Wayne Gretzky is, Dad." At least I'm pretty sure I do. "What does that have to do with anything?"

"It means that if you never try, you're gonna fail a hundred percent of the time."

"But what if I do try, and I still fail?"

"Then at least you know you tried."

That seems like little consolation. This theory has holes. Hockey is stupid.

"Dad, I just need to figure out if she likes me or not, without looking like a total idiot."

"Well," he says, "do you have physical contact? Does she touch your arm or your shoulder, that kind of thing?"

Is my dad getting girl advice from one of Beth's magazines?

"Yeah, she's touched me on the arm a couple of times."

"Does she laugh at your jokes, even when they're not funny? Which I'm guessing is most of the time?"

"Dad!" I say, smacking his arm. "Yeah, she laughs at my stupid jokes."

"Does she talk about other guys in front of you? Other guys she might be interested in?"

I have to think about this for a second. "No, not that I can remember."

"That's a very good sign. Women don't talk about other guys in front of guys they're interested in." He looks at me and grins. "Michael Jordan said that."

I laugh. That was a good one. And this may actually be the longest conversation I've ever had with my dad. More importantly, I think he'll finally stop reading so much into my pink Cons.

The phone rings in the car and Dad picks up on speakerphone. It's Mom.

"Ray, I just wanted to see if you dropped Chuck off yet."

"Not yet. He's still in the car with me. We were just chatting."

"*Oh, hi, honey!*"

No need to yell . . .

"Hi, Mom."

"What are you two talking about?" she asks. Does she really need to know everything?

"Nothing, Molly," Dad says, winking at me. "Just guy stuff."

I'm in my room after school, Facebook chatting with Steve. He claims Wendy wasn't wearing any underwear today. Steve really needs to get out more.

I get a text and assume that Steve is sending me some sort of grainy, inappropriate picture message. But it's not Steve; it's Amy. She says she made something for me and wants to bring it over. I tell Steve I'll BRB, then close the chat window, reply to Amy, and try not to hyperventilate.

Twenty minutes later, Mom yells from downstairs, *"Chuck, your friend is here!"* And next thing I know, Amy is entering my bedroom holding a box in one hand.

"Guess who I brought!" she says. I hear something, but hope it's not true. I pray it's not true. But there she is: Buttercup, on a leash, walking behind Amy. Amy, wonder-ful, beautiful, perfect-in-every-way Amy, has brought a dog. Into. My. Bedroom.

She lets Buttercup off her leash and the dog immediately makes a beeline for me. I think I might pass out. Buttercup stops and licks my socks. I'm not even wearing Cons—everything is happening so fast.

Amy gives me a hug and a kiss on the cheek. "Hey, Chuck!" she says. The cheek kiss is new. My brain is chugging on all cylinders.

I manage a "Hi" and we sit on my bed—where no girl has gone before. Buttercup thankfully seems a lot more docile than she was the last time I saw her. After losing interest in me, she lies in one spot on the floor, watching us with her big brown eyes. As long as she remains stationary, and away from me, I think I can handle it. I keep a silent inventory of everything the dog touches so that I can disinfect it later.

"I hope you don't mind," Amy says. "My parents aren't home and I didn't want to leave her all alone."

"It's okay," I say meekly, and I'm pretty sure my voice cracks, seventh-grade style.

Amy puts the box in my hands. "So," she says, "I was thinking. You've been so amazing, helping me with calc and everything. And since you're so sweet, I decided to make *you* something sweet. Check 'em out."

I open the box. There are four cupcakes inside. Each one has a different formula written in frosting:

$$\int a \, dx$$

$$\int e^x \, dx$$

$$\int a^x \, dx$$

$$\int \ln x \, dx$$

She made me antiderivative cupcakes.

"Since you like math, you're gonna *love* these," Amy says.

I'm speechless. It's the nicest thing anyone has ever done for anyone, ever.

"Well?" she says.

"This is awesome. You didn't have to do this."

"I wanted to. Try one!"

I reach into the box and pick up a cupcake. I don't know if I make a weird sound or a weird motion or what, but something spooks Buttercup and she starts jumping around my room, slobbering and shedding everywhere. I start to feel nonexistent hives forming on the back of my neck again.

Amy reaches into the box and grabs a cupcake as well. I have one eye on the cupcake in my hand and the other on Buttercup. Every fiber of my being is focused on not freaking out.

I peel the cupcake wrapper away, a task that millions upon millions of normal teenagers do every day without even a second thought. My fingers sink into the spongy bottom of the cupcake. I feel a lump in my throat. Amy is already munching away. She licks her lips, which in any other scenario would be the hottest thing of all time.

Hold it together, Chuck. Hold it together.

I manage to take a bite. I can't even taste anything. Buttercup is sniffing at the door of my closet, behind which lies my absurdly massive collection of Cons.

"Do you like it?" Amy asks.

"Yeah," I say, trying to act convincing. "It's great."

"Good, I'm glad."

My hands are starting to shake. I can feel cupcake crumbs and frosting on my lips and on my fingers. I have goose bumps everywhere. I feel itchy.

Act normal. Act normal. ACT NORMAL!

I feel like I might throw up. *That dog smell. It's in my room.*

"Are you okay?" Amy asks.

"Yeah," I say, "just a little hot." And cold. *At the same time.*

"Anyway," Amy says, "thanks again for everything." She smiles at me. I feel my eyes start to water. *Must wash hands.*

"Okay" is all I can muster.

Suddenly, Buttercup loses interest in my closet, bounds over to me, and jumps up into my lap. I have no choice but to quickly put my cupcake back in the box and put the box beside me—right on my fucking bed. Buttercup is in my arms in a flash.

Amy giggles. "She doesn't usually like boys."

Amy looks at me. Her eyes are so blue. I look at her. Something is happening.

Buttercup starts to lick the frosting and crumbs off of my fingers.

THERE IS A FUCKING DOG ON MY FUCKING BED LICKING FUCKING FOOD OFF MY FUCKING HANDS.

"Aww, I've never seen her do that before," Amy says.

My back is soaked with sweat.

She looks me in the eyes.

She licks her lips.

She closes her eyes.

She moves her face toward mine.

I can't take it anymore.

I lose it.

I jump up from the bed just before Amy's lips touch mine, tossing Buttercup onto the floor and accidentally knocking over the box in the process. Buttercup lands in the open box, squishing the remaining cupcakes with a yelp. I run out of my room and into the bathroom in the hallway.

I throw the faucet on full blast and plunge my hands and face into the water. I pump the soap dispenser furiously. My mind goes blank. The soap and the anxiety meet in the middle like a battle scene from *Braveheart*.

The soap slowly begins to win out. After what seems like an eternity of scrubbing, I regain consciousness. I realize what I just did. *Oh shit.*

I dry off and scurry back into my room. Amy has cleaned up the cupcake box and put the leash back on Buttercup. She's crying. It occurs to me that she still looks beautiful.

"Amy . . ."

She struggles to speak through the tears. "Don't ever talk to me again."

"But . . ." I stammer.

She sobs. A great big, sad sob. My heart feels like it has ceased pumping.

She grabs the box and the leash and blows past me out of my room, Buttercup in tow. I can still hear her sniffling as she goes downstairs and leaves my house.

I start to cry, too.

I started taking the Lexapro."

"Excuse me?" Dr. S. says, removing her glasses. I don't think I've ever seen her do that before.

"I started taking the Lexapro," I repeat.

"When?"

"A couple days ago."

She puts her glasses back on and starts to scribble in her stupid notepad.

"I'm glad to hear that, Chuck. May I ask why you had a change of heart?"

"I dunno," I murmur, and shrug my shoulders. I don't really feel like talking.

"Is everything okay? Did you get into an argument with your parents?"

"No."

"Again, Chuck, I'm glad you've decided to take this step. But it would be helpful to find out *why*?"

I close my eyes. I wish I was somewhere else. I wish I

was some*one* else. I take a couple of medium-sized breaths. I rub my eyes. I open them.

Nope. Still in Dr. S.'s office. Still Chuck Taylor: Professional Asshole.

I rub my eyes some more.

"Chuck? Are you sure you're okay?"

"I just want to get better," I finally mumble.

"You just want to get better?"

I hate when people repeat what I just said!

"Yeah, I just want to get better. Whatever I have to do."

"So there was no specific incident that made you change your mind?"

First she wanted me to take the fucking Lexapro, now I decide to take it and she grills me on *why*? Leave. Me. Alone.

Dr. S. finally interprets my silence correctly and moves on.

"Well, Chuck, it will take at least a week for the medication to start having any effect, at which point we can attempt some CBT and try to beat this once and for all, yes?"

"Whatever."

"Do you have any questions about the medication?"

I squeeze my fists together tightly. I just want to leave. The Incident with Amy was the worst moment of my life. Just thinking about it makes me shiver. Poor Amy. I threw her dog and her cupcakes on the floor and ran out of the room when she tried to kiss me. I'd hate me, too. Worst of all, I can't even enjoy the fact that Amy actually *wanted* to kiss me because I fucking ruined it. Now she won't even look at me in class. It's like her first day all over again.

"I Googled it," I say. I can't even muster the energy to utter more than one sentence at a time.

"You Googled Lexapro?" Dr. S. asks.

"Yeah."

One of the first things that came up? That there might be "sexual side effects." No problem there! Why does the universe taunt me?

"I read," I continue, "that some of the side effects could be insomnia and anxiety and, like, other bad stuff."

"That's true, in some instances?" Dr. S. says.

"Well, aren't those all the things I'm trying to get rid of? That makes no sense."

"In the short term, Chuck, you may feel an uptick in your existing symptoms. But in the long run, hopefully, you should start to feel some relief?"

I'm confused and I'm angry and I'm frustrated, but most of all I'm kicking myself. I should have tried to get better sooner. I shouldn't have been such a pussy. Then maybe I wouldn't have screwed everything up with Amy. Now I'm taking weird drugs that may possibly make me even crazier, but it doesn't even matter because she's gone. I know I need to somehow get her back, but I can't do that if I'm acting like a raving lunatic. So I decided to take the stupid pills.

"Is there anything else you'd like to ask, Chuck?"

I just stare at my Cons. These are the only pair in my collection where the color and the emotion actually happen to make sense together. I nervously tap my sneakers against the floor.

They're black: depressed.

HH HH HH
HH HH HH
II

I stare at my food without touching it. Steve looks at me like he's trying to figure out what to say.

We're sitting at our table in the cafeteria alone. Kanha got sick again in Calc this morning and went home afterwards. Either he's allergic to integrals or he keeps getting food poisoning. This time I didn't laugh when he threw up. Amy didn't even turn around.

"Come on, Chuck," Steve says. "We've been over this. You'll get Amy back. It was just a misunderstanding."

"It wasn't a misunderstanding. She thinks I'm a freak. I *am* a freak."

"No, you're not."

"Steve, what you would do if you tried to kiss me and instead I threw your dog on the floor?"

Steve isn't quite sure how to respond to that. Perhaps it's not the best example.

"Look," Steve says, "you always say how cool Amy is. So you should just go talk to her."

"She said she never wants to speak to me again."

"Girls always say that."

I look up at Steve, calling him out.

"Girls always say that . . . according to the many movies and television shows I've watched on the matter," he clarifies.

"I can't," I grumble. "I don't even know what I would say."

"Try texting her."

"I did. No response."

"Oh."

I *have* sent Amy a few texts. Sure it's a little informal given the circumstances, but I can't get up the nerve to call her and I know she won't pick up anyway. Plus, I wasn't lying when I told Steve I didn't know what to say. I swore I would never tell her about my, well, mental issues. My first text was beyond lame: *So sorry about other day. Pls call me. Tell buttercup I said hi.* She didn't write back. I don't blame her.

"What about Facebook?" Steve asks. "What have her statuses been like?"

"I don't know," I say. "She defriended me."

"Ouch."

"Actually I can't even see her page at all now."

"So she blocked you?"

"I guess so," I admit.

"Shit," Steve says, scratching his head. He looks genuinely concerned.

I yawn for like the tenth time at lunch and Steve takes note.

"Did you sleep at all last night?"

I've been taking the Lexapro for about a week but haven't

told Steve about it. I don't feel any less OCD-ish. Still checking the stove, making lists, and keeping embarrassingly detailed records about my masturbation regimen. I do, however, feel kind of sluggish. I'm sleeping slightly better—not because I don't have the urge to get up to pee fifteen times—but because I'm so exhausted. The weird thing is, even though I'm sleeping more, I feel even more tired during the day. These pills are strange. I hope Dr. S. knows what she's doing.

I pick at my food. "Yeah, I slept," I say.

"You wanna hang after school?" Steve asks.

"I don't know, maybe."

I don't really want to do much of anything. I feel very *blah*. And I miss Amy's laugh—with me, at me, whatever. I also haven't told Steve that I never put in a good word for him with Beth. I know he's chomping at the bit to ask me about it but won't say anything while he knows I'm wallowing in my own misery.

"Kanha sent me a text before," Steve says, trying anything to get my mind off Amy. "He wrote: *Can't stop yacking yo. I gots to check myself.*"

Steve's impression of Kanha is spot-on. My first instinct is to think about how much Amy will laugh when I tell her about it. Then I remember that's not gonna happen. I look down at my untouched food.

Steve seems worried.

HHT HHT HHT
HHT HHT HHT
III

I have become a cartoon character.

I'm literally hiding behind a bookshelf in the library, peering at Amy through an opening in the books. I'm toeing the line between spying and stalking. Neither, I realize, is very becoming.

Amy isn't sitting at our "usual" table, which is unoccupied. Instead she's sitting at a much smaller table a few feet away. It's so small there's really only room for one person. I assume this is not a coincidence.

As I'm gathering up the nerve to approach her, the situation takes on an additional, unwanted element: Ashley Allen. *What the fuck is he doing here?*

He walks by Amy's table and stops to say something to her. I've never seen them interact before (or ever even seen Ashley in the library before, come to think of it), but I'm too far away to hear anything. I glance up at what section I'm in. It's Women's Studies. Even the Dewey decimal system is mocking me.

Amy is craning her neck to look up at Ashley, he's so fucking tall. Whatever he says, it makes Amy smile. I feel myself involuntarily smiling as well, which makes me feel even worse.

At last, Ashley walks away and Amy goes back to her books. That seemed like a friendly chat, which enrages me. Was Ashley . . . hitting on her?

I struggle to compose myself and finally do. I try to think of all the nice times me and Amy spent together. She let me try on her camouflage jacket. She picked an eyelash off my cheek and asked me to make a wish (guess what I wished for). She made me calculus themed cupcakes. *She tried to kiss me.* I decide it's time to talk to her face-to-face.

I take a roundabout route to get from where I'm hiding to Amy's table, hoping to avoid her seeing me for as long as possible. She spots me about ten feet away. I think she frowns. I mean, I've never really seen her frown before, but it *looks* like a frown. At least she doesn't get up and run away or blow a rape whistle or anything.

I get to her table.

"Hey," I say.

"Hey," she says back.

This is about as far into the conversation as I've planned ahead of time. I'm a fucking idiot. I'll have to improvise from here.

"Can I sit?"

Amy just shrugs.

I pull up a nearby chair and sit across from her, but the table is so small that I'm uncomfortably close to her. If you were gonna devise the most awkward configuration possible in which to have a conversation with a girl who has recently shunned you, this would be it.

I notice she's looking at her calc textbook, picking up right where we left off. Not even missing a beat without good ol' Chuck.

"Amy."

"Yeah?"

"I'm sorry about what happened."

"Don't worry about it."

This response baffles me. So does that mean she doesn't hate me? Why are girls so *confusing*?

"So . . ." I say.

"You really hurt my feelings, Chuck," Amy jumps in. "I'm totally humiliated. I feel like an idiot. And Buttercup got really scared."

"I know, I know. I'm sorry," I say.

"I don't know what happened or why you did that, but I just think it's better if we not be friends anymore."

Hearing Amy say that in the heat of the moment at my house is one thing. Hearing her say it a week and a half later when we're both calm is much, much worse. I want to tell Amy about my "condition." I want to tell her that cycles in my brain get stuck on repeat and that a dog licking frosting off my hand causes a chemical reaction that I can't control—so much so that I'm actually seeing a shrink and taking *drugs* just to try to fix it. But I can't do it. She'll think I'm a psychopath. She'll *definitely* never talk to me again.

"But," I stammer, "can't we just forget what happened? Like, start over?"

"Chuck," she says, "I wish we could. But we can't. What

happened, happened. I know you're a good guy, but I can't look at you the same way after that. I put myself out there and you were just so . . . *mean*."

Amy starts packing up her books.

No one has ever called me mean before. I've been called loser, weirdo, fuckface. None of which hurt more than when Amy Huntington called me mean.

"I wasn't trying to be," I say. "I just . . ."

Amy stands up and looks at me, presumably expecting some sort of explanation.

"I'm just sorry, Amy."

She frowns again. Definitely a frown. "Goodbye, Chuck," she says.

She walks away, her ballet flats barely making a sound on the carpet in the library.

The stove is off. The stove is off. The stove is off.

I'm lying in bed, desperately fighting the urge to get up, go downstairs, and check the burner thingies. I checked them before bed. I put my hand on each burner and all four were cold to the touch. I stared at the knobs. They were all turned to Off. I listened and smelled for gas. No surprise there—my parents' electric stove did not in fact sound or smell like gas. It's definitely off. O-F-F off.

I can't tell if the Lexapro is working. The sluggishness has pretty much worn off. But I can't tell if it's, like, made me feel less crazy or not. Dr. S. keeps saying that I should try CBT when I feel like I can handle it. I don't know. Maybe the Lexapro is working, because this is the first time I even feel like I can sorta maybe try it.

It's hard. Much harder than I thought. All I have to do is not check the stove.

It's off. It's definitely off. Mom and Dad didn't even cook tonight. But I can't help but wonder if I checked all the burners. Did I do it right? Did one of them feel a little warmer than the others? Was one of the knobs slightly askew? I should really check again. What's two minutes of getting out of bed to double/triple/quadruple check just to make sure my family doesn't die in a fire? *Must fight it . . .*

My alarm clock blares. Ugh. It's so fucking early. I don't *wanna* go to school. Wait a minute. Wait just a minute. I didn't check the stove. I did it! I leap out of bed. I come downstairs. Mom, Dad, and Beth are all eating cereal. They haven't been burned to death.

"Morning, honey," Mom says.

I ignore her. I head for the stove. I check the burners. Still off. I stare at the knobs. *Still off.* I get that rush that comes with checking and rechecking. But it feels ever so slightly different this time. It feels . . . kinda *stupid*.

A few days after my modest stove triumph, I'm at my locker. The bell has rung. I'm already gonna be late for class. My locker is still open. I know that once I close it, I'll want to turn the lock fourteen times. I've tried to CBT that sucker after every period so far, with no luck. This is my last class of the day. *Close your locker, spin it once.* I put my hand on my locker. I feel the familiar sensation that precedes one of my compulsions. *Must fight it . . .*

I slam my locker shut. I spin the lock once. I quickly jump back a few steps. Had anyone seen me they'd think I'd just trapped a wild animal in there. I stare at my locker. I know it's locked. There's no way it *can't* be locked. I force my feet to move. I walk away, keeping my eyes fixed on the locker. I finally reach a corner. I turn. I jog away, victorious.

A few days go by. I'm walking from lunch to my next class. I just ate a sandwich. To the naked eye, my hands are pristine. Not a crumb, not a drop of mayo. But *I* can feel it. I try to tell myself that even if my hands *are* dirty, it's not a big deal. I watch the other, normal kids leave the cafeteria. Not one washes their hands. They're not going to die of *E. coli* and neither am I. *Act like a human being.* Go to class, Chuck. It's just bread. Your hands are fine. *Must fight it . . .*

I pass a hand sanitizer dispenser. It calls to me. A chill crawls up my spine. I look at my hands. They're clean. *They're clean.* I rub my fingers together. *They're not clean.* I give in. I head to the hand sanitizer. It squirts onto my hands. I spread it all around. It feels amazing. But I also feel a little guilty. And discouraged. I have a long way to go.

I heard they're canceling Senior Weekend."

"What?" Me and Steve are driving to school and what he's just said causes me to nearly gasp.

"Yup, apparently there's some problem with the permits for the campgrounds, so they're just canceling it. I saw some kids talking about it on Facebook."

"Steve, are you serious?"

He looks at me and grins. "April Fools!"

"What?"

"It's April 1st, Chuck. I'm just fucking with you."

Goddamnit, Steve.

"Oh," I say, slumping in the passenger seat.

"Would you really be that excited if Senior Weekend got canceled?"

"Of course," I say. "Then I wouldn't feel so bad about not going, and I'd know Amy isn't spending the night in the middle of a field somewhere with Ashley Allen."

"Chuck, you saw them talking once. I'm sure it's nothing."

"I guess," I admit.

"So listen," Steve continues, "Kanha's brother is still home from college for spring break. He told Kanha he'd get us some beer as long as we can hide it until the camping trip."

"Steve, how many times do I have to tell you? I'm not going. And we don't even drink."

Last year, me, Steve, and Kanha waited outside the deli for like an hour begging people to buy us beer. Some guy finally did and we drank it in Steve's basement while his parents were out for the night. I hated the taste, Steve fell asleep, and Kanha, of course, threw up.

"I thought you were, like, working on some of your shit," Steve says.

I still haven't told Steve I'm taking Lexapro but I did tell him a little bit about CBT. He was bound to figure out that I was acting stranger than usual—or is it *less* strange?—sooner or later.

"Yeah, I'm working on it," I say. "But it's one thing to try not to wash my hands, it's another thing to sleep on grass and take a shit in a hole."

"We're not sleeping on grass and shitting in holes. You're gonna sleep in a tent, and there are bathrooms, Chuck. I'm sure there's even Wi-Fi. The campgrounds are like two miles away. We're not going to the fucking Amazon."

"I don't want to talk about it anymore."

"Fine," Steve says in a huff. "Don't go. But I'm telling you right now, I *am* going to prom whether you go or not. I'm not missing everything."

"And who are you going to go *with*?" I ask.

"I don't know yet, but the guys are starting to ask the

girls. I don't care if I have to get a mail-order bride, I *will* go. And, actually, I Googled it and they're not that bad—"

"Steve!"

"What?"

"You're not ordering your prom date from the Internet. I don't even know why you want to go so bad anyway. It's so corporate."

"Corporate?" Steve mocks. "Did you just say that prom is *corporate*? What does that even mean? Who says that?"

"I don't know. It's just stupid is all."

Only a few weeks ago, my grand plan was to take Amy to prom. That would be the crowning moment of my otherwise pitiful high school career. It actually seemed like it could happen, too. But clearly I fucked that up big-time. As much progress as I'm making with my OCD, I'm going the opposite direction with Amy. Winning her back now seems more daunting than befriending her was in the first place.

Senior Weekend is ruined. Prom is ruined. Me and Amy are ruined. Everything is ruined. My only solace is in an orange pill bottle sitting in a drawer next to a sheet full of tally marks.

All I want to do right now is concentrate on studying for the AP exams and stop imagining Steve putting a corsage on a hooker.

HHT HHT HHT
HHT HHT HHT
HHT I

O kay, Number Thirteen, it's just me and you."
I'm in the elevator in Dr. S.'s building, talking out
loud to myself like a crazy person. Mom is out shopping
with Beth and Dad is swamped with tax season so I came by
myself. There's no one around to press the elevator button
and I've resolved not to push it with my elbow like I've
done in the past.

*It's just a cycle in your brain, Chuck. Nothing is gonna happen
if you touch the button. Press it and you'll see.*

I quickly press it. I stab it, really. It lights up and we're
off. That's one of the techniques I've been trying to use
in my CBT—just do something real quick before I have a
chance to talk myself out of it. It works about half the time.

I stare at my finger. It *seems* gross. But I try to remind
myself it's fine. It's so hard. I feel like a fraud in my brown
Cons: I'm definitely not as confident as I was when I put
them on.

* * *

Dr. S. has been in a much better mood in the past few weeks since I started taking the Lexapro. Which is good. It's really awful when you think your shrink hates you.

I give her the update. Dr. S. said I should concentrate on one thing and take it slowly, but I feel like I want to tackle everything at once and just cure myself. Plus, with a certain female companion avoiding me like the plague, I have plenty of free time to work on my rituals.

"The stove and my locker are where I'm doing the best, I think. I haven't gotten out of bed to check the burners at all this week. And I'm pretty good at turning my lock just once. *And* I pressed the elevator button coming up here." I proudly hold up my finger like I just voted in an Iraqi election.

"That's great, Chuck. I'm thrilled to hear you're making progress. How about your urination issue?"

"Uh. I'm still getting out of bed to pee a lot even though I don't have to."

"And the hand washing?"

"Yeah . . . still doing a lot of hand washing. And list making. And knocking on wood. And walking the same route in school . . ." I start to trail off.

"Chuck, don't get down on yourself. You're making excellent progress for such a short period of time? This will not be fast or easy."

Dr. S. has been pounding that into my head for weeks: *This will not be fast or easy.* I mean, it's fucking discouraging. I'm taking the medication. I'm doing what she tells me to do. Why won't this just go away?

"OCD won't just go away, Chuck?"

For a second I think Dr. S. has read my mind. She's on point today.

"I know," I say. "But I wish it would."

"The process of habituation—"

I know what Dr. S. is gonna say so I break in with my own impersonation of her, complete with Indian accent: "—takes time. You're retraining your brain, yes?"

I grimace a bit. Did I just offend her? Then, Dr. S. smiles.

"Yes, exactly. I guess I do sound a little like a broken record?"

I shrug in agreement. "A little."

Dr. S. nods and continues smiling. I *am* pretty funny sometimes. She puts her notepad down.

"So what do your parents think about your progress?"

"They're relieved I think. Mom doesn't really ask me because she knows I get annoyed. So I tell my dad and he passes it on, usually getting most of it wrong."

Dr. S. grins again. I'm on a roll.

"And how does Amy feel about it?"

I forget to breathe for a second. She catches me off guard with that question. Things with Amy haven't changed. When she sees me, she looks away. If we make eye contact and she has no other choice, she'll give me a little half-hearted hello nod. We haven't spoken or texted or Face-booked or sent smoke signals since the Incident. I think maybe it's time to tell Dr. S. what's going on.

"Me and Amy had a fight," I say haltingly. "I sorta did some stupid things and now she hates me. That's why I started taking the Lexapro."

"I'm sorry to hear that, Chuck?"

"I should have listened to you. If I had tried some of this stuff sooner, maybe she wouldn't have found out I'm all, well, messed up."

Dr. S. chooses not to acknowledge this statement. "I had a feeling something was wrong. You haven't mentioned her in a while?"

"Yeah, well, I haven't talked to her in a while. But now that I'm taking the Lexapro and I'm getting better, I'll show her that I'm not some weirdo. I'm gonna get better for her."

"Chuck?"

I wait for her to say more. Every once in a while her random question mark insertion still throws me for a loop.

She finally continues: "This is very important. What you are doing is admirable? But you have to want to get better for you. From what you've told me about Amy she seems like a really great girl, yes? But I'd be worried if you are basing your recovery on the actions of someone else. You are the one who suffers from this disorder and you are the only one who can beat it. It's a part of you. This is your fight? It's all about you."

I nod my head obediently. What Dr. S. is saying makes sense, I guess. But who are we kidding? It's all about Amy.

I think she's crying and I don't know why.

I'm standing down the hall from Amy's locker, which is in the sophomore hallway because that's all that was available. I've begun to watch Amy a lot from here, occasionally having to scurry away either when I think she sees me, or if Beth (who I avoid in school at all costs) is in the vicinity.

I'm far enough away to feel safe, and from here I'm pretty sure Amy is crying. She takes tissue after tissue from her purse and wipes her face and nose. The scene of course brings back a lot of bad memories. The last time I saw Amy crying was the Incident. I didn't like it then and I sure as hell don't like it now. *If I only knew why.*

Suddenly, Stacey and Wendy appear on the scene like a couple of vultures. I think they are trying to console her. I start to run through any reasons I can come up with of why Amy would be crying. Did she fail a test? Nah, she gets straight A's and would never be that upset over a test.

Is she moving again? But she said she was gonna be in town for a while! Maybe it's, like, her time of the month or something. Though that never made her cry when we were hanging out together. Is she crying about . . . me? What the F is going on?

Amy turns around—but doesn't see me—and I finally catch a clear glimpse of her face. Yup, definitely crying. Her face is all red. Her bangs are all over the place. She hugs Stacey and then closes her locker. All three of them start to walk in my direction. Still perplexed, I haul ass outta there.

Steve texts me that he knows what happened and will tell me at lunch. I'm sick with anticipation. Finally he gets to the table where me and Kanha are sitting.

"Well?" I ask, before he even has a chance to sit down.

"Barry and Barry have AP Chem with Amy," Steve says. "They told me she said something about her dog running away."

"*What?*" I exclaim.

"Yeah, they said she said her mom was taking it for a walk and it got off the leash or something and ran away."

"You're telling me Buttercup ran away?"

"Is that his name? Then I guess so."

"It's a she."

"What?"

"Buttercup. She's a she. Not a he."

"Oh," Steve says, "well then, yeah, *she* ran away."

"When did this happen?" I ask.

"Today I guess," Steve says.

I run my hands through my hair. This is intense. I have mixed feelings. On one hand, Buttercup is the root of all evil. She's the reason I freaked out. She's the reason Amy hates me. On the other hand, Amy loves that fucking dog. I mean, she *loves* it. She must be devastated. I wish there was something I could do.

Kanha senses I'm not dealing with this well. "You okay, dog?" He immediately realizes this is a poor choice of slang. "Uh, sorry," he quickly adds.

"Yeah, I'm okay I guess," I say. "Did you hear anything else, Steve?"

"That's about it. He—sorry, *she*—is wearing a collar, but unless she comes back on her own or someone finds her, there's not much they can do."

I imagine Amy coming home from school today and not being greeted by Buttercup running out of the doggy door. I want to cheer her up, make her laugh, do *something*.

But, as usual, I'm helpless.

The whole point of this therapy, Dr. S. keeps telling me, is to get used to the anxiety of *not* doing my compulsions so that, eventually, I'll get acclimated and won't feel the anxiety anymore in the first place. Supposedly, the Lexapro cuts down on my initial anxiety just enough for me to try the therapy. Sometimes I think it's working and sometimes I don't. Right now I'm having a tough time.

I'm lying in bed, trying not to pee. I peed for a while before I went to bed. It was a good, nice long pee that I had been saving up. I shook it out real good. My bladder is empty. But I've only been in bed for eight minutes and I already feel like I need to pee again. I feel like just maybe I didn't get it all and if I don't get up and pee again, I may never fall asleep.

I try not to think about it. I think about Amy instead. Even though Dr. S. says I need to do this for me, I still can't help but envision the moment when I tell Amy I'm cured—that I'm no longer a dog-hating nutcase. That's gonna be a great day. I wonder if Amy is up, too, thinking about Buttercup. She's probably looking out her bedroom window all sad and shit.

I start thinking about peeing again. Just pee once, quickly. It will be fine. No. I can't give in. I roll over on my stomach. That seems to help a little.

I dream I'm skipping rocks on a pond with Amy, only the pond is the top of a cupcake.

I wake up. It's morning. I didn't get up to pee the whole night! I can't remember the last time I ever did that. I roll out of bed just as my alarm goes off. Now I *do* have to pee. It feels great.

Rocking green Cons today: hopeful.

It's warm outside. Student government is having a bake sale in front of the school. Stacey is manning one of the tables. I'll have to handle money, touch food, and interact with Stacey. A trifecta of challenges. I'm in.

I approach the table. Stacey smiles at me politely, but I know she just wants my cash. "Hey, Stacey," I say. She seems surprised to realize I possess the power of speech.

She goes into pitch mode: "Would you like to help the class raise money for Senior Weekend?"

Ah, so this is for the Senior Weekend. Add that to the list of triggers I'm now facing. What's one more than a trifecta? A quadfecta? Whatever, stop stalling.

I look at all the cookies and brownies. I search for the least messy-looking one. I hear Dr. S. admonishing me in my head. *This won't be fast or easy.* I decide to go for the sloppiest one instead. There's some sort of coffee cake–looking thing that's all crumbly.

"I'll take that one," I say with relative authority.

"That'll be $2.50," Stacey says.

I glance at her cleavage. Sweet mother. The guys are gonna have a field day with those in college.

I take a five out of my wallet. I can smell the grime on it. I sense the ink rubbing off on my fingers. I hand it to Stacey. Her finger grazes mine, something she definitely doesn't even notice but that adds a *fifth* element to this challenge because I hate touching other people's hands. She gives me back the two most beat-up singles I've ever seen and two quarters. I hesitate for a second. Coins are the grossest! I sense Stacey anointing me Patron Saint of Weirdness.

"Thanks," I say, pocketing the money, taking a deep breath, and then picking up the piece of cake. I try to distract myself by asking Stacey a question. "Have you heard anything about Buttercup?"

"What?" Stacey says, seeming annoyed for no reason.

"Amy's dog. Do you know if she found it?"

"Oh. No. Still missing. Amy is putting up flyers."

"Oh. Okay. Thanks."

Stacey displays a "do you realize how painful this is for me?" fake grin. I take it as my cue to leave.

I lean on the wall, across the hall from a hand sanitizer dispenser. So far today I've spoken to Stacey Simpson for the first time since eighth-grade Home Ec and contributed money to the god-awful Senior Weekend. Neither killed me. I touched Stacey's finger, handled money, *and* ate the piece of cake. I haven't washed my hands yet. Dr. S. wants me to expose myself to my triggers, well that's what I'm doing.

I feel the sugar and crumbs and ink crawl up my arms from my fingers toward my face. *You're fine, Chuck. It's just food. It's just money. It's just some hot chick's finger. You'll be fine.*

The hand sanitizer is so tempting. It's calling to me.

I take a step toward it.

I fight back.

I don't give in.

I walk away.

I win.

I'm gonna do this.

I'm staring at my computer screen. The link that used to be Amy's Facebook profile now just reads:

The page you requested was not found.
You may have clicked an expired link or mistyped the address. Some web addresses are case sensitive.

I didn't mistype shit. Amy still has me blocked. This is getting ridiculous. I need to talk to her. We're in freakin' Calc together every day and she hasn't said a word to me in weeks.

I start to think: if Dr. S. and Steve are fine with playing the Amy card, then why can't I do the same thing? I know what I'm gonna do: I'm gonna play the Buttercup card.

I grab my phone and send Amy a text: *I heard about Buttercup. Are you ok?* It's a sensitive subject, but I know it's the only thing that Amy will definitely respond to. She can't ignore this.

Sure enough, Amy texts back a minute later: *Thx. I'm sad.*

Three words, one of which isn't even real, and that's the most substantial conversation I've had with her since we talked in the library. I don't have much to go on.

I respond: *Is there anything I can do?*

She writes back: *No. Thx.*

Compared to the witty banter we used to have at our usual table, this is plain painful. I start to think it's a lost cause.

I write: *I'm sorry again about what happened.*

It takes a little longer for her to write back this time. But she finally responds: *It's ok.*

I was expecting a little more than that. I wonder if maybe she wrote more, then deleted it and just sent that. The good news is that she doesn't really seem to be mad anymore about what happened. The bad news is that I think she's just too upset about Buttercup to care about anything else.

It's time to go for broke. I told Dr. S. and I told myself that I would never tell Amy what's wrong with me. But the truth is, she knows *something* is wrong with me. As Dr. S. says, OCD is a part of me. Amy is the coolest human being I have ever encountered. She'll understand. I hope.

I type very deliberately. I read it over. I hit send: *Amy, I have ocd.*

There, it's out there.

She writes back like two seconds later. It just reads: *?*

I write back: *Obsessive-compulsive disorder.*

She responds: *I know what it is. Why r u telling me?*

Now I'm typing at warp speed: *That's why I freaked out. But I'm trying to get better.*

She writes back: *Oh, Chuck*.

Oh, Chuck?

I have no idea what that means. Damn you, text messaging, and your lack of inflection! Is it "Oh, Chuck" as in oh, *that's* what's wrong with you? Or is it "Oh, Chuck" as in oh, you sad, pathetic creature?

My phone pings. It's another text from Amy. Two in a row. I read it and then bury my face in my hands.

It says: *I have a little ocd too.*

Oh Amy, Amy, Amy. Sure, you're neat and have all of your notebooks for school labeled and organized. But you carry half-eaten granola bars in a dog hair–covered backpack and wear a jacket that's been God knows where. You're not OCD, any more than Steve is.

I decide not to write back even though I've finally engaged Amy in what passes for back-and-forth between us these days. I played the Buttercup card *and* the OCD card; that's enough for one night. But as much as I'm disappointed by Amy's response, I'm starting to realize what she's thinking. She had some asshole boyfriend in San Diego. All she cares about in the world is her dog. She finally meets a new guy—me. That guy not only turns out to be an asshole, too, but fucks with the dog as well. Double whammy. When I told her that I have OCD and she responded, "So do I," that tells me one thing—Amy doesn't understand what I'm going through. She's just confused. I mean, who the hell wouldn't be? But, as Mom would say, that's great.

How the hell is that great? Because now I know what's wrong and how to fix it.

Me and Steve are studying in the library. It's the last place I want to be right now, but AP exams are rapidly approaching and we need to get our shit together. Just to prove the world hates me, the only available table is me and Amy's usual one. I swear I can still smell Amy's scent hanging in the air. It smells like baby powder and awesomeness.

Of course, I'm too distracted to get any work done.

"So I think I know what to do about Amy," I say.

Steve looks up from his books. "Oh yeah?" he offers.

Steve is no doubt getting sick and tired of hearing me talk about Amy. He's a trouper as always, though, and plays along. "What are you gonna do?"

"I'm just going to tell her everything. About Dr. S., about Lexapro."

"Wait, what?"

Shit. I realize that I never even told Steve that I was taking Lexapro.

"What the fuck is Lexapro?"

"It's just this drug that Dr. S. put me on. It helps with my OCD stuff."

"How long have you been taking it?"

"Like a month or so."

"How come you didn't tell me?"

"I don't know. It's embarrassing. I didn't want you to think I was strange or anything."

Steve looks at me. "Chuck, you're literally the strangest person on earth."

We both laugh. There's no denying that.

"So, anyway," Steve says, mercifully moving on, "you're gonna tell Amy all that why?"

"She still doesn't understand why I freaked out. But I think as long as she knows, and knows I'm getting better, she'll finally start hanging out with me again."

"Okay," Steve says, "that sounds like a plan."

He doesn't seem very convinced, but I know it's the right thing to do.

"I mean, if I can't get her to come to prom with me," I say, "I don't know what I'm gonna do, you know?"

"Yeah, Chuck, I get it."

Definitely getting sick of me.

"So, speaking of girls . . ." Steve says gingerly, "you never told me what happened with Beth."

"Huh?" I *really* don't want to go there.

"Beth. Your sister? You said you were gonna put in a good word for me. Remember, right after that bullshit with Parker?"

Of course I remember. But I hoped, however unlikely, that Steve hadn't.

"I didn't want to say anything since you were dealing with all this shit," Steve continues, "but now that you're doing better and taking some fancy-schmancy medication, maybe you could tell your best friend Steve what happened when you talked to Beth?"

I don't know what the best move is here. Do I tell Steve that I never even really talked to Beth about him because there's no way in a million years she'd ever go out with him (which I'm totally fine with)? Or do I sugarcoat it?

"Uh," I stammer, and begin to improvise, "I did talk to her." Steve is literally on the edge of his seat. *Amy's* seat, actually. "I talked to her for like two seconds. She said she'd think about it."

"What?" Steve asks excitedly. "So you told Beth I was interested and she said she'd *think about* it?"

"Yup," I say, as if answering quickly makes it any less of a lie.

"That's great news!" Steve says. "That means there's a possibility, right?"

"Well," I say, "I mean, there's always a *possibility*. But to put it in math terms, the expected value is not very high."

"Still, *some* chance is better than *no* chance," Steve says, getting even more excited.

This is exactly the kind of giddy reaction I was worried about.

"Thanks so much, Chuck. I really appreciate it. I mean, think about it, if I date your sister that would make us, like, brothers! Sort of."

"Yeah," I say. "Brothers." I shudder at the thought of Steve with Beth. "We should get back to work."

Steve is bopping his shoulders and doing a little dance in his seat while he cracks open a study guide. I've made my best friend's day. What could possibly be wrong with that?

W ell, Chuck, from what you've told me, you seem to be making remarkable progress, yes? You've attempted CBT on a number of your compulsions and in many cases succeeded in reducing your symptoms. We still have a very long way to go, but I'm encouraged by your improvement and would like to keep you on Lexapro for the time being?"

I nod my head glumly as Dr. S. continues.

"However, I can't help but notice that your mood has been somewhat . . . unpredictable in our last session or two. Are you not pleased with your progress, Chuck?"

"No," I say, "I'm okay with how things are going. I've just got some, like, other things I'm dealing with."

"That's quite all right, Chuck. What's on your mind?"

While taking the Lexapro and working at CBT and actually seeing some improvement has been great, it's also had a weird side effect: my brain feels a little clearer. And that means I've been spending more and more time thinking about high school ending and my life, well, still sucking.

"My best friend . . ." I begin.

"Steve?"

"Yeah, Steve." I still always forget that Dr. S. is paid to listen and remember what I tell her. "Steve has liked my sister forever. And even though Beth is the worst, I told Steve that I talked to her about him, you know, put in a good word or whatever."

"And this bothers you because of your relationship with Beth?"

"No, it bothers me because I never actually said anything to her and I lied to Steve."

"Oh." Dr. S. looks at her notepad. I see a very brief glimpse of the judgey/disappointed face she's so good at suppressing when we talk.

"Well, there is one way you can address this I think?" she continues.

"There is?"

"Why don't you try *actually* talking to Beth?"

I suddenly realize what she means.

"I get it. So if I *do* talk to her, then—technically speaking—I never lied to Steve!"

Dr. S. shakes her head. She seems amused. "That's not exactly what I meant, Chuck. I'm merely suggesting that if and when you do talk to Steve about this, it might benefit you to know Beth's true feelings first, yes?"

Damn. And here I thought Dr. S. was being all devious and telling me a way out of this mess. That's no help at all. *Beth's true feelings?* You don't need a color-coded Converse system for that. Her only mood is bitch.

"Do you understand what I'm saying, Chuck?"

"I guess so."

"What else is troubling you?"

"Are we really supposed to be talking about this stuff? Like, non-mental stuff?"

"I'm a psychiatrist, Chuck. I'm not just here to treat your OCD; I'm here for your overall well-being. I assume this has to do with Amy?"

"Yeah," I admit.

"Having healthy relationships is an integral part of mental health. I will do my best to help. Think of me as, what do you call it? Your 'wingman'?"

Did my shrink just call herself my *wingman*?

"My wingman?"

"Yes, your wingman. That's the term, correct?"

"Yeah . . ." I laugh to myself and am momentarily thrown off. "Okay, so I've told you about Amy before. Things haven't exactly been going well. I'm thinking about just telling her everything. Maybe sending her an email. Tell her about you, about the Lexapro, all of it."

"Uh huh," Dr. S. says.

"And then," I continue, "ask her to prom."

Dr. S. wrinkles her forehead in surprise.

"Really?"

"Yup."

"Isn't the prom not until June?"

"Yeah, but people are starting to ask."

"That's a bold move, Chuck. Something you never would have considered when you first started coming here?"

That's definitely true. I never would have asked any girl to prom the way I was a few months ago. Dr. S.—and

Amy—have changed all that. I have no idea what Amy will say, or if she'll even listen to me long enough for me to ask her in the first place, but it's the only thing I can think of to show her how I feel once and for all.

"Well," Dr. S. says, "if it doesn't work, then at least you know you tried?"

Dr. S. doesn't seem very optimistic about my plan. In fact, she sounds a little too much like Wayne Gretzky for my taste. She puts her pen down and smiles.

"We're out of time," she says.

Soon, I will be too.

HH HH HH
HH HH HH
HH HH II

I walk into my bedroom and am struck by déjà vu. Beth is using my laptop, which she knows she's not allowed to do. Just a few years ago, this exact scene played out and it led directly to my bizarre Converse system. *Angry = red Cons.* It seems like so long ago.

"Beth, what the hell are you doing in here?"

She turns around—busted.

"My computer is dead."

"Then plug it in, idiot."

"Something is wrong with the charger."

"That's not my problem. Get outta here!"

"Just let me do one more thing. Please?"

I sense an opportunity.

"Fine," I say.

"Really?"

"Yeah, five minutes."

"Okay, thanks."

She turns back to my computer and I sit on the bed and

take off my gray Cons. I can't believe I've been doing this for *years* now. My system is one of the few compulsions (along with my beat-off tally) that I haven't told Dr. S. about or tried CBT on. Some things are just too weird.

I look over and see that Beth is on Facebook. Obviously what she's doing is not *that* important. It annoys me that I'm actually hesitant to talk to my own *younger* sister.

"Beth," I say, "can I talk to you while you're doing that?" Before she even has a chance to bitch me out I add: "You know, since you're on *my* computer and all?"

"Fine, what?" she sighs.

I try my technique of speaking without thinking: "Steve likes you."

Beth doesn't even stop typing.

"What?"

"Steve. He really likes you."

Now she turns her head toward me.

"Steve Sludgelacker likes me? Like, *likes* me likes me?"

"Yeah."

She doesn't say anything for a moment. But for a second, I think I see a flicker of an ounce of half a smile. I mean, who doesn't enjoy being told that someone likes them?

"Ew, gross," she says finally, and turns back around.

"That's it? That's all you're gonna say?"

"What do you want me to say, Chuck? So your weirdo best friend likes me. Big deal."

"Well, what do you think about him?"

"What part of 'Ew, gross' do you not understand?"

"Why don't you just think about it? Even for a day." *That way I technically didn't lie to Steve.*

"Think about what?"

"You know," I say, "think about if maybe you could possibly like him, too."

She turns her head again. "Is this a joke?"

"No, I just—"

Then Beth drops a bomb: "I'm going to the prom with Parker."

"Wait, what?" I'm flabbergasted.

"Parker asked me to the prom yesterday and I said yes. That's who I'm talking to right now."

"That's what was so important that you had to use my computer?"

She ignores me and turns back. It feels wrong that words that Parker is typing are going through the Internet and appearing on *my* computer screen. I feel like he's right in my bedroom, stupid warm-up pants and all.

"But you're only a sophomore," I say, still trying to make sense of everything.

"So? Sophomores sometimes go to prom."

"Are you and Parker . . . dating?"

"No. I mean, not really."

I don't know what that means and, honestly, I don't even want to know. Beth finally logs off and closes my laptop. Instead of merely patronizing me by turning her head again, she swivels around completely so that we're actually facing each other.

"Look," she says, "Steve seems like a really great guy. He's always nice to me. I actually just accepted the friend request he sent me a few years ago."

"A few *years* ago? He said he requested you a few *months* ago." Apparently I'm not the only one telling white lies.

"And I know that Parker can be a dick sometimes."

Now that's the understatement of the year.

"But I think he's cool," she continues, "and I really wanna go to prom. So I'm going with him. Obviously I can't date someone else." She stands up. "I guess just tell Steve I'm sorry."

She goes to leave my room.

"Hey, Beth," I say.

"Yeah?"

"Did you accept *my* friend request?"

She looks at me quizzically. "Nah," she says, walking out the door. "I rejected you a long time ago."

Beth Taylor certainly knows how to make an exit.

Me, Steve, and Kanha are taking a break from studying for APs and getting some food at the deli a few blocks from the high school.

"Remember when we got that dude to buy us beer here last year?" Kanha says.

"Yeah, and then you threw up all over my basement," Steve replies.

"Why you gotta bring that up, dog? I was lit *up*."

"You had half a beer," I say.

Me and Steve have a laugh at Kanha's expense. The deli guy brings our sandwiches to our table along with one paper-thin napkin each.

"You want me to get some more napkins?" Steve asks.

"Nah," I say, digging in. My hands are messy, of course, but I can just, like, *deal* with it better now. One napkin is enough. Steve is legitimately impressed.

For a while, the only sound is rabid chewing. We've been studying like crazy and everyone is starving. Finally, Steve chimes in.

"I think Parker is gonna kill me before I even get to take the APs."

"What are you talking about?" I say.

"He slipped a note into my locker today. It said 'You're gonna die, Fudge Packer.'"

"Are you kidding me? How do you know it was Parker?" I say stupidly.

"Who else would put that kind of note in my locker? Plus, he spelled 'die' D-Y-E."

We all have to chuckle at that.

"Why didn't you say anything before?" I ask.

"I don't know," Steve says. "I guess I'm just used to it. He's full of shit anyway."

"That's not cool, dog," Kanha says. "You gots to tell Mrs. Rodriguez."

"Nah, if I tell on him, that's just gonna make things worse. Besides, I also got some good news: Beth accepted my friend request yesterday!"

"Oh snap! For reals?"

Steve and Kanha high-five.

"Yup," Steve says. "It's all because of Chuck. He said he would put a word in, and he did."

"Let's not get carried away, Steve," I say. "Just because she accepted your friend request doesn't necessarily *mean* anything."

"It means *something*," Steve says. "It can't just be a co-incidence. And that's also why I'm not gonna go tell on Parker. I'm gonna get back at him somehow. I'm gonna do it for Beth. I'm gonna show her I'm not some pushover. I'm gonna . . . I'm gonna take her to prom!"

This is getting out of hand.

"Steve," I say, "I don't want you to get too excited. Beth is very . . . indecisive."

"She won't be indecisive when I take Parker down."

"First of all, how exactly are you gonna do that? And second of all, if you want to get back at Parker, that's something you gotta do for you, not for Beth."

It strikes me that I sound exactly like Dr. S.

"Hey, Taylor, don't be raining on Sludgelacker's parade, yo."

Leave it to Kanha to inject some common sense into the proceedings.

"I just don't want Steve to get his ass kicked—physically or, you know . . . by my sister."

"I'll be fine," Steve says.

I'm not very confident this is true and am eager to start talking about something other than Beth before I dig myself an even bigger hole.

"So, I wrote a whole email that I'm sending to Amy tonight. I'm gonna tell her everything and explain everything and tell her how I feel. Then I'm gonna meet her in the library tomorrow and ask *her* to prom. This is my last chance to make things right."

They don't say anything but Kanha reluctantly takes a few dollars out of his pocket and hands them to Steve.

"What's that for?" I ask.

"I bet Kanha that you couldn't go one conversation without bringing up Amy," Steve says.

"Are you serious?"

"Yeah, Chuck. It's getting a little ridiculous."

I'm annoyed and embarrassed. But most of all, I feel the urge to get some more napkins.

Wearing tan Cons—anxious—and the same pair I wore the first time I met Amy at this very table. It's been less than two and a half months but it feels like two and a half years. Last night I poured my heart out in an email to Amy. I told her everything, even including a link to the Wikipedia article on OCD, and she agreed to meet me here.

Amy arrives. She hasn't worn her camouflage jacket in a while. It's almost May and it's been pretty warm. It's a shame; I love that jacket. She sits.

"Hey."

"Hey," I respond.

She brushes her hair out of her eyes. Gets me every time. I don't know where to start. Luckily, she does.

"That was some email you sent me."

"Yeah. Sorry about that."

"There's no need to apologize. I'm glad you sent it. You've obviously been dealing with some serious stuff. It explains a lot, that's for sure."

"So you forgive me?"

"Chuck, I'm not mad at you. You're like the sweetest, most down-to-earth guy I've ever met."

Am I really "down to earth"? Amy has this way with words that just makes me feel so good about myself.

"And," she continues, "you're gonna make some girl feel really special one day."

No, no, no, no, don't give me this "some girl" crap!

"But, Amy—"

"Chuck, you're going through a lot, but so am I. I just moved here, now we're almost graduating, I'm still waiting to hear back from colleges, I'm taking a million classes, Buttercup . . ."

She trails off. I think she might break down. She gathers herself and continues.

"Buttercup is gone, I just got out of an awful relationship, I just don't know if I can deal with this right now."

"But," I plead, "everything was going so great until that day at my house."

"It's not about that anymore, Chuck. I like you. I really do. You have such a kind heart."

A kind heart? Who says things like that? Amy Huntington, that's who.

"But I just have so much going on right now, and judging from that email, so do you."

This is backfiring . . .

"But, Amy, I'm getting better! You should see how much better I'm doing! I don't make lists anymore. I walk down whatever hallway I want."

"That's great, Chuck. It really is."

"Don't you see? I did it because of you. I'm doing it *for* you."

"And that's honestly amazing," Amy says. "But this is something you have to do for yourself, Chuck. Not for me."

She sounds like Dr. S. lecturing me, and me lecturing Steve. I have a knot in my stomach and it's throbbing and I feel like I'm shaking. I can't undo what's happened no matter how hard I try, no matter how much I *want* to.

"You said it yourself in that email," Amy continues, "you have a long way to go. But I'm just not in a place where I can be more than friends with you. It wouldn't be fair to either of us. You still have so much to do—and I know you can do it—but I can't put myself out there again. It's too much."

I say, "I understand," but the truth is I *don't* understand.

Amy puts her hands on mine. All I can think about is how close we came to kissing. I decide there's one more thing I have to say.

"Will you go to the prom with me?"

Amy withdraws her hands.

"What?"

"Will you go to prom with me? At least as friends?"

"Chuck," she says with a sigh.

"I know you think it's all 'corporate' and everything but—"

"Ashley already asked me."

I feel like I've just been clobbered in the face. My vision goes blurry for a second.

"What do you *mean* Ashley already asked you?" I'm starting to sound like a whiny bitch but I don't care.

"He asked me a few days ago."

"What did you say?"

"I said I wasn't sure I was going."

What's the smallest thing ever? A nano-something? That's the size of the breath of relief I take. A nano-breath. Ashley asked Amy to prom but she didn't say yes yet. That's all I've got to hang on to right now. I'm pathetic.

"You know how I feel about prom," Amy says. "The camping trip in a month—*that* I'm going to. But I just don't know about prom."

"But I was hoping . . ."

"I'm sorry, Chuck. I was gonna tell you. It's just simpler this way. Just like I said the first time we ever hung out—I try not to get attached. Someone always gets hurt."

Of all the scenarios I considered about how this meeting would go, none were as bad as what is actually happening. I want to close my eyes and go back to before I knew Amy, when I was still super OCD but at least didn't have a hole in my chest where my aorta and the rest of my heart used to be.

"Listen," she says, "I have to go. I'm helping my mom put up some more missing-dog flyers."

"Okay," I mumble, "I guess I'll see you in class." My one solace: first-period Calc and getting to stare at the back of Amy's head every day.

"There is no more class, remember? Cimaglia's giving us the week off to study independently for the exam."

"Oh. Right," I say.

"And after the AP, I'm not gonna be back in class either. I have to sit in on another Spanish class to make sure I can pass the final and graduate on time."

"Oh," I say again, now barely audible.

"I'll see you around, Chuck," she says, standing up and grabbing her backpack.

She smiles at me before turning and leaving.

It's the first time she's ever smiled at me that I didn't smile back.

After staring into space for what seems like hours, I need every ounce of willpower in my body to finally get out of my seat in the library. Also the library is closing and the janitor kicks me out.

I walk through the near-empty school for a while. The school that has given me nothing but grief in return for all the hours of my life I've spent in it. I'm continuing to wander aimlessly when I hear something strange, like someone is choking. I follow the sound, turn a corner, and find the source: Parker has Steve in a headlock in the middle of a deserted hallway.

I immediately look to see if there's anyone to help, but no one is around. My heart pounding, I yell out (or, rather, speak sorta sternly): "Hey!"

Parker looks up and sees me but doesn't react. He just continues to keep Steve in a headlock. It doesn't seem like he's actually choking Steve, more like just humiliating him by not letting go. I approach them.

"Come on, Parker, just let him go."

Parker actually releases Steve and I think perhaps I've somehow defused the situation. Then he *shoves* Steve into the lockers. Like, *hard*. Steve's shoulder hits the lockers and the only thing that keeps him from collapsing to the ground is that Parker is grabbing on to his shirt, stretching out the collar.

"What are you gonna do about it, Chuck?"

I know this is gonna sound absolutely fucking crazy, but my first reaction is that I can't believe Parker even knows my name. What an awful thing to think at a time like this.

"I *said*, what are you gonna do about it, Chuck?"

Parker slams Steve into the lockers again, even harder. Steve is starting to tear up. This is getting serious.

"Just leave him alone," I say. "What's your problem?" What is Parker's problem anyway? He's been picking on Steve since he moved to Plainville for seemingly no reason.

"He's a fudge packer, *that's* my problem. He deserves to get his ass kicked."

Oh, well thank you for that very thoughtful response, Parker. That really explains a lot.

"Can't you just pick on someone else?"

"Who, like you?"

Parker slams Steve into the lockers again, this time letting him fall to the ground. Parker looks me up and down. *Oh shit.*

"Well," Parker grunts, "I could kick *your* ass, but then your sister would get all upset."

"My sister?" I say, puzzled. The day's events have fried my brain.

"Yeah, your sister," Parker says. "You know, the chick I drive to school every day? The one I'm taking to prom?"

Steve is doubled over on the ground, but there's no way he didn't hear that. I'll have to deal with that later, though.

I don't say anything.

"Why don't you give me your best shot," Parker says.

"What?"

"I'm sure Beth would be okay with it if *you* hit *me*, right?" He turns his face sideways as if he's giving me a target.

I'm totally mystified. I mean, does he *want* me to hit him? How can he be so dumb at life yet so good at soccer and mind games?

I just stand there.

"Your best friend is on the floor and you won't even take a free shot at me? Pussy."

Without saying another word, Parker turns around and walks away in the other direction. With their flair for exits, I can almost see how he and my sister could make a good couple.

I rush to Steve's side and help him up.

"Are you okay?"

"Yeah," Steve says, wiping away the tears. "It looked worse than it was."

"It looked pretty bad, man. We need to tell the principal."

"No. I'm fine."

"You sure?"

"What was Parker talking about? About driving Beth to school and taking her to prom?"

The kid just got beat up in the hallway and this is what

he wants to talk about? I thought I'd have more time to prepare.

"I don't know, Steve. That was weird."

"Chuck, you know you're the worst liar ever, why do you even try?"

Well, not the *worst* liar ever. After all, I did convince him I put in a word with Beth when I hadn't yet, *and* I kinda left out some pertinent information at the deli . . . but that's neither here nor there.

"It's true," I admit. "Parker has been driving Beth to school."

"So you never talked to her about me?"

"No, I did."

"And?"

"She said she was going to the prom with him."

"You knew all this and you didn't tell me?"

"Well, I mean . . ."

"So you lied to me."

"Not technically, I—"

"You're such an *asshole*, Chuck."

"Steve, listen—"

"No. I ask you to do one thing, *one thing* for me, and you lie to my face about it? You make me look like an idiot?"

"I'm sorry, man. I've just been dealing with all this Amy stuff. And she just told me she doesn't want to be with me and—"

"Enough! *Shut the fuck up!*"

Steve has never, ever raised his voice in the entire time I've known him.

"All you fucking do is talk about Amy. Amy this, Amy that.

Meanwhile, *I'm* the one getting my ass kicked every week and do you do anything about it? You're seeing a shrink, you're dealing with your shit, and I always have your back. But do you have mine? No. You don't help me when I ask you to. You lie to me. You're a fucking terrible friend."

"Steve . . ."

"Fuck you, Chuck."

Steve's face is bright red. He has fresh tears in his eyes and his nose is running. At this very moment, I'm actually a little afraid of him. But I also know (or at least *hope*) that he's merely caught up in the moment. He doesn't say anything else. He just walks away in the opposite direction of Parker, holding the shoulder that just got bashed into the lockers.

I'm left all by myself, in more ways than one.

So, Chuck," Dr. S. smiles optimistically, "how have you been doing this week? Any new victories to report?"

"Nope," I say flatly.

"And why is that?" she says, still grinning.

"Because I stopped taking the Lexapro."

"Excuse me?"

"I stopped taking the Lexapro."

"Chuck, are you joking?"

"Nope," I say again, matter-of-factly.

"What happened? What's wrong?"

"Life sucks, the drugs aren't working. Fuck it. I don't give a shit."

"Is this about you and Amy?"

"There is no me and Amy. And there's barely a me and Steve."

"So you and Steve had a falling-out?"

"Yeah, thanks for that advice, Doc. You're a great wingman."

"Chuck, your tone concerns me. This is the first time I've ever seen you so . . . angry?"

"Why shouldn't I be angry? Me and Amy are through. My only friend in the entire world is mad at me. I haven't said a word to either of them in days."

Dr. S. gets all delicate and shit: "I understand you're having a tough time. But your symptoms were still getting better, yes? Why discontinue the medication? Now is the perfect opportunity to put your recovery to the test."

"I just don't wanna take it anymore. It's stupid."

"Chuck, I can't stress enough that discontinuing medication like Lexapro 'cold turkey' can potentially be dangerous? The drug affects your brain chemistry and you need to be weaned off of it properly."

"I don't care."

"Abruptly stopping Lexapro has been known to cause depression, anxiety, insomnia—"

"Wait a minute," I interrupt. "Those were all the side effects of *taking* the drug."

"This is true, yes?"

"So how can the side effects of taking it be the same as what it treats *and* what happens if I *stop* taking it? That doesn't make any fucking sense!"

My head is spinning.

"Chuck, please try to watch your language?"

I don't want to be here anymore. My sessions with Dr. S. have coincided with the worst months of my already awful life. True, my symptoms were getting better, much better in fact. But I don't care if they come back. I can already feel them starting to creep back, and I only stopped taking the pills a few days ago. It almost feels like a relief—like something familiar that I've been missing.

"Choosing whether or not to take the medication is your decision," Dr. S. continues, "but your parents and I will have to monitor you closely. I also must say again that I *strongly* recommend continuing this course of treatment?"

"So what?"

"Chuck, I promise you that whatever is going on in your life, you can deal with it. You're a stronger young man than you realize. You've come so far, yes?"

"Look where it got me," I say. "No one likes me. Who cares if I count how many times I jerk off?"

"What was that?"

I remember that I never even told Dr. S. about my tally, now proudly entering its seventeenth month and counting.

"Nothing," I say. "I don't wanna take the Lexapro anymore. I don't wanna do CBT anymore. I just want to be left alone."

Next month is graduation. It's so tantalizingly close. I just want to suffer in peace and then get the motherfuck out of this town.

"Perhaps we should consider different medication? There's a variety of—"

"Why do you wear sneakers?" I blurt out, cutting off Dr. S. again and trying to talk about something, *anything* other than medication.

"What?"

"Why do you wear sneakers? You don't think it's weird? You're a shrink."

"Psychiatrist."

"Whatever. Why do you wear sneakers? It's weird."

"Because they're comfortable, Chuck. Why do you wear sneakers?"

Dr. S. seems to be getting a little irritated.

I stare down at my red Cons. I think about how they're so much more than just sneakers to me.

"I have my reasons," I mutter.

I swear this is the last day I'm ever gonna think about math for the rest of my life. The Calc AP exam has finally arrived and I can't wait to get it over with. It's not going to be easy, though—and I don't just mean the test.

I'm sitting in a classroom in West Lake Elementary, where the exam is being administered. Obviously I don't do well in unfamiliar environments, especially since I stopped taking the Lexapro. To make matters worse, in one corner of the room is Steve, doing his best to ignore me, and in the other corner of the room is Amy. I can't remember the last time I saw Amy, considering we haven't had Cimaglia's class and her locker is in fucking Siberia.

The weather has been weird all year and early May is no exception—it's hot as balls. Amy turns to talk to a friend (I remember when she didn't know anybody . . .) and I notice something startling about her face: she has freckles! I guess the sun or the heat or whatever makes them come out. It's so weird to see her like that. I want to say something about them, poke fun, ask her about them, laugh about it, anything, but she's also doing her best to ignore me.

The test isn't for another twenty minutes. I have to pee. I think I could probably hold it in but then I know that's all I'll be thinking about during the exam. I walk to the front of the room and approach the proctor.

"Where's the bathroom?" I ask.

"Down the hall and to the right," she says. "But you're gonna need this to get in."

She hands me a giant black binder clip that has a key attached to it. A bathroom key? Seriously?

OCD thoughts swarm my brain: people holding the key, touching the bathroom door, going to the bathroom, touching the toilet handle, touching the bathroom sink, urine and shit and grossness everywhere. I hesitate.

The proctor stands there, key in hand, wondering what the hell is wrong with me. Finally I just grab it without thinking and scamper out of the classroom. When I get into the hallway, I put the binder clip between my elbow and my side so I don't have to touch it with my hands. Just weeks ago I might have been able to deal with this. Not anymore.

I take a piss, displaying almost acrobatic abilities to touch everything in the bathroom with my feet and elbows. I wrap the key in paper towels and stick it back in my side. Then I scrub my hands clean.

I'm about to leave the bathroom when I decide to take a second. The enormity of the moment strikes me. I don't know if I'm prepared for this exam. Since the Incident I've dreaded studying calc because it reminds me of Amy. But I *have* to do well so I can place out of calculus in college and never see an antiderivative for as long as I live. I also realize that I'm standing in a bathroom with a key wrapped in paper towels lodged in my armpit. My symptoms are coming back faster than I expected. I'm feeling claustrophobic. I have to get outta here.

I manage to exit the bathroom without touching the doorknob with my hands, and then lean against a nearby wall, trying to catch my breath. In moments like this, Steve would always be there to calm me down. Not today. And that's when I look down the hallway and see her: Mom.

For a second I'm totally confused, before I realize this is where Mom works. I went to Plainville Elementary, and have never been inside this building before, so I guess I just didn't put two and two together. Mom seems surprised too as she approaches.

"Chuck? What are you doing here?"

"This is where the AP exam is."

"*Oh, right.* They're administering some of the exams here because of overflow at the high school."

"Yeah."

"It's so nice to see you. Are you ready for the test?"

"I'm a little nervous."

Mom and Dad have been walking on eggshells around me ever since Dr. S. informed them I stopped taking my medication. It's weird, though, because I feel like Mom has become slightly less annoying lately. I don't know if she's laying low, or if I just kinda subconsciously need her more than ever.

"You're gonna do great, honey."

She musses my hair and gives me a kiss on the forehead. That always makes me feel better.

"Thanks, Mom."

"I have to get to class—and you need to kick some butt on that exam."

"Okay."

"Good luck and let me know how it goes."

"I will, Mom."

"I love you."

"I love you, too."

She leaves and I head back to the classroom. It occurs to me that either Mom didn't notice the ball of paper towels wedged in my armpit, or she just chose not to say anything.

The test is going well, much better than I expected. Tutoring Amy *has* helped me after all. Every time I come across a topic me and her went over together, I remember a conversation we had or a joke we shared, and I can recall exactly what we were studying at the time. I slyly glance over at Amy, as if she'll feel some sort of connection. She never reciprocates. Steve is sitting behind me so I can't tell what the hell he's doing.

Before I know it, the exam—and (hopefully) my calculus career—are mercifully over. I won't get the results until July. I seek out Kanha, knowing he's the only one here I can go over the answers with.

Two weeks of AP exams are finished, so the lockers in the senior hallway have taken on a party atmosphere. For anyone in AP classes, high school is basically over. For anyone not in AP classes, well, let's face it, they never gave a shit to begin with. All everyone is talking about is Senior Weekend, which is only three weeks away. There's only one person who really understands how I feel right now.

I wander the hallways after school, trying to find Steve. He's not at his locker, but his car is still in the parking lot. Steve doesn't give me a ride anymore and I missed the bus home, so I have to wait until the late bus anyway.

I end up in the hallway where Parker smashed Steve into the lockers. I wish I had done more but I know that if I could go back, I'd probably do the same thing—next to nothing. I hear a sound coming from the other end of the hallway. No, it's not Steve getting choked again—it's laughter. Obnoxious, halting, nasal laughter. I trace the sound to a classroom with its door open a crack and peek inside.

It's a meeting of the Mathletes. There's Steve, seated between Barry and Barry, chatting away. I instantly know what Steve is telling everyone about: his hand job. Those nerds are eating it up.

Steve glances over and happens to spot me peeking in. I quickly duck away, but I hear him tell the group he'll be right back. He comes outside and approaches me in the hallway.

"What are you doing?" he asks accusingly.

"Nothing," I say. "I missed the bus."

My attempt to make Steve feel guilty fails miserably.

"So you joined Mathletes?" I say, hoping somehow it's not true.

"Yup. There's one more meet this year and they were down a man."

"Oh."

"Is that a problem?" Steve says.

"No. I just . . ." I have nothing else to say. I stare at my feet.

"Okay, well then I'm gonna go—"

"Are you ever gonna talk to me again?"

"I don't know, Chuck. Maybe it's time we moved on."

"What does that mean?"

"It means we're going off to college soon. We're not even gonna be in the same state anymore. And I need to meet new people and have friends that will stick up for me, and listen to me when I have problems."

"How many times have I listened to that fucking story about your stupid hand job?" I say. "It's not even true. You're such a liar."

My face is starting to get red. So is Steve's. Two losers girlishly emoting in the hallway.

"It's not about that and you know it," Steve says. "And who are you to call *me* a liar? You lied to my face and I had to hear about it while I was beat up and on the ground. You think that was fun?"

"No, of course not. But—"

"I can't do this anymore, Chuck. I can't waste my life standing around while you scrub your hands and complain about some girl."

"Steve, I'll make up for it. I'll talk to Beth. I'll—"

"Forget it, man. It's too late."

"But . . . what am I supposed to do now?" I plead.

"I don't know, Chuck. But you know what's coming up? A little camping trip called Senior Weekend. I'm gonna be there. Those guys in there," he says, gesturing toward the Mathletes meeting, "they're all gonna be there, too. You know who else is gonna be there? Parker. He's probably gonna beat me to a bloody pulp and leave me to die in the woods. But you know what? I don't care. The question is, Chuck—where are *you* gonna be?"

I don't say anything. My mouth is completely dry.

"I thought so," Steve says. "Do me a favor, don't talk to me anymore." He shakes his head dismissively and walks back into the classroom, slamming the door behind him.

I can't believe my best friend just broke up with me.

HHH HHH HHH
HHH HHH HHH
HHH HHH HHH
IIII

O ne, two, three, four, five, six, seven, eight, nine, ten, eleven, twelve, thirteen, fourteen. One, two, three, four, five, six, seven, eight, nine, ten, eleven, twelve, thirteen, fourteen. One, two, three, four, five, six, seven, eight, nine, ten, eleven, twelve, thirteen, fourteen.

I'm standing at my locker like a zombie, spinning my lock over and over again. I can't get it to feel right. When I hit fourteen it just doesn't feel the way it used to. The Lexapros must have scrambled my brain or something. Things seem worse now. Much worse. The last few weeks are just a haze.

On maybe the twentieth try I finally get it right and start to walk to my next class. Everything around me seems so dull—and I don't mean dull like "boring," I mean dull like, not sharp. Colors are drab and sounds are muffled. I don't feel right at all.

Stacey and Wendy walk by me going the other direction. All I can hear is the word "limo" and I know they're talking about prom. It just adds to the lingering headache I've had for days now.

I spot a hand sanitizer dispenser and make a beeline for it. I haven't even touched anything—*anything*—since my last squirt, but even the air feels contaminated these days. It's the hand sanitizer near the gym, where I introduced Amy to Steve (or, rather, he introduced himself). It's also where I dicked Steve over for the first time. I guess you could say this very spot is where my downfall began.

I slowly rub the sanitizer into my hands, savoring every last tingle—my only remaining pleasure. I absentmindedly look at the wall outside the gym. It's the PWLJFKHS Sports Hall of Fame. It's filled with old black-and-white photos of athletes with short shorts and mullets. I imagine a Biggest Reject Hall of Fame or Shittiest High School Experience Lifetime Achievement Award. That's the only way I'd ever be memorialized in this godforsaken place.

I continue on, slowly, to class. Out of the corner of my eye, I spot a flash of red. It's Amy, though I only see her for a split second before she disappears from view. I notice my body has very little reaction. Such a sighting used to stop me dead in my tracks while annoyed classmates swerved to avoid me. Now: nothing.

I walk past the cafeteria and remember the first time I tried to CBT my way out of washing my hands after I ate a sandwich. I failed that day but eventually figured it out. I haven't done any CBT for a while now. Don't plan on doing any anytime soon.

I decide I'm not going to class after all. I've never missed a class in my entire life. Never even been sick. I guess that's one of the benefits of constantly washing your hands and being addicted to sanitizer. There's a first for everything, though. I walk outside. There are a few kids eating or just hanging out on their lunch period. I stand right where the table was where Stacey sold me that piece of cake. I haven't been eating much lately.

I look up. There's not a cloud in the sky. It hasn't rained in forever. Dad had the Weather Channel on yesterday and I heard some shitty weather might be coming next week. I think about how little effect it will have on my life. Rain, no rain, whatever. It doesn't matter.

I step on a flyer that's lying on the ground. It reads:

SENIOR WEEKEND—
DON'T MISS IT!

I remember seeing a similar flyer when I was a freshman, and asking Steve what Senior Weekend was. I remember when I cared.

My dad looks ridiculous sitting in a little plastic chair that's meant for a five-year-old. He keeps shifting his weight and crossing his legs to try to get comfortable. Finally he turns the chair around and rests his arms on the back. That seems to work better.

"Chuck, are you listening to what Dr. Srinivasan is saying?"

Not really.

Me, Mom, and Dad are sitting in Dr. S.'s office for an "emergency" meeting about my "condition." Apparently, it's been called so hastily that there wasn't even enough time to get an extra chair for my dad, so he just grabbed a kiddy one from the waiting room.

Since I went off the Lexapro, I've still been seeing Dr. S. every week, though I mostly keep quiet—just like in our very first session. At home, Mom and Dad have been keeping increasingly close tabs on me, namely asking "How are you feeling?" on a nearly hourly basis.

"Chuck?" Mom says again.

"Yeah, yeah, I'm listening," I say.

"We're all worried about you. Dr. Srinivasan really feels like you should go back on the medication."

"I'm fine, Mom."

"Chuck, you've been moping around the house for weeks. I think you're depressed. Ray, what do you think?"

Dad shrugs. "He seems pretty depressed to me."

Thanks for that profound second opinion, Dad. It's just so hard to take him seriously while he's sitting in that little chair.

"Chuck," Dr. S. says, "have you been experiencing mood swings? Have you been feeling generally down lately?"

"Not really," I mutter.

Is it a lie? I don't even know. I feel like shit. I have nothing to look forward to. But when did I ever *not* feel this way?

"Mrs. Taylor, this is a completely normal reaction to Chuck's discontinuation of the Lexapro?"

"I don't know, is it?" Mom responds.

I chuckle. Then I laugh—like really *laugh*. I think it's the first time I've actually laughed out loud since . . . since reminiscing with Steve and Kanha at the deli. Mom, Dad, and Dr. S. all look at me, puzzled.

"That wasn't a question, Mom," I snicker.

"What?" she says.

I laugh again.

Mom and Dad obviously haven't spent as much time talking to Dr. S. as I have. Mom doesn't realize Dr. S. wasn't *asking* her if I'm having a normal reaction, she was *telling* her.

"Nothing, forget it," I say.

Just demonstrating that I still have the ability to laugh seems to cut the tension in the room, at least for the moment.

"Chuck," Dr. S. says, "I understand you've had a difficult few months. But you've also had a great deal of success, yes? It would be a shame to throw it all away."

"Chuck," Mom adds, "you're going away to college soon and we're not gonna . . . well, be able to keep as close an eye on you anymore. We just want to make sure you're okay before you leave."

"Chuck," Dad chimes in, "all we're saying is that—"

"*Enough!*" I yell, startling everyone. "I'm fine! Yeah, maybe I'm a little depressed. Who wouldn't be? My sorta kinda girlfriend broke up with me. My best friend hates me. High school is ending. It is what it is. I don't like the way the Lexapro makes me feel and I don't like CBT and I don't like coming here. I just don't wanna do it anymore. But I'll be okay. I promise."

Everyone else in the room trades doubtful glances.

I turn to my parents. "Can we just leave?" I plead.

I look at Dr. S., then quickly look away. I feel like I've let her down. But really I just want to go home.

She smiles at me reassuringly. "Remember, Chuck, whether or not you get better is up to you."

I think it's the most declarative statement she's ever made.

Then, for good measure, she adds: "Yes?"

I'm vegging out on the couch in the living room, watching TV. It feels good to be doing absolutely nothing (though "good" is a relative term these days). As if on cue, Beth, the devil's spawn herself, appears and sits down next to me on the couch.

"What are you doing?" she asks.

"What does it look like I'm doing?"

Beth shrugs. "Mom says you haven't been feeling well."

"Yeah well Mom says a lot of stuff."

We both sit quietly for a while.

"Wait a minute," I say, turning to Beth. "Did Mom send you to check up on me?"

"I don't know."

Beth is a worse liar than I am.

"You can report back to Mom that I'm fine."

"Actually," Beth says after pausing, "there's also something I wanted to tell you."

"If you broke my laptop again I'm gonna seriously kill you," I say.

"I didn't break your stupid laptop. I wanted to tell you that I'm going on the camping trip tomorrow."

"What?" I say, annoyed and disbelieving.

"I'm going to Senior Weekend," Beth repeats.

"What do you mean you're going to Senior Weekend?"

"Parker asked me to go with him so I'm going."

"But it's *Senior* Weekend! This isn't like prom. You're not *allowed* to go."

"Who says?"

It's that cavalier attitude that I secretly envy in Beth. She just doesn't give a fuck.

"There's no way Mom and Dad are gonna let you go," I say confidently.

"They already said I could."

"Are you kidding? How?"

"I told them it's a school event and there are gonna be adults there and all my friends are going."

"But none of that's true, Beth!"

"Well, duh." She rolls her eyes.

An evil genius, that's what my sister is.

As I'm attempting to process everything, I have a thought that makes me shudder.

"Wait . . . you're gonna share a tent with Parker Goldberg?"

"No," she says. "What do you think, I'm some kind of slut?"

I've honestly never thought of her in *any* way involving anything like that. Gross.

"I borrowed a tent from the Greulichs," Beth says. "They have all kinds of crap in their garage."

I think about our elderly next-door neighbors. All they ever seem to do is sit outside their house, forcing me to wave whenever I come home. Who knows what they have in that garage.

"Anyway, I just wanted to let you know I'm going," she adds.

The fact that my *sophomore* sister is going to *Senior* Weekend—but I'm not—is so annoying, so outrageous, so *unfair* that I don't even know what to do with myself. I imagine Beth getting eaten by a bear in the woods. Literally being torn limb from limb while she screams.

Suddenly, there's a huge thunderclap outside. The lights flicker and me and Beth jump. That shitty weather is finally here. I can't help but feel bad about Beth and the bear, and knock on my knee accordingly.

"So how come Steve doesn't pick you up for school anymore?" Beth asks, deftly yet painfully changing the subject.

I was sitting on the couch, minding my own business, and now Beth reminds me that I'm the only senior taking the bus in the history of high school. Thanks, thanks a lot.

"I don't know; he just doesn't."

"Do you, like, want me to ask Parker if he can take you? He has room."

There's no prize, no plaque, no announcement, no fanfare. However, I'm fully aware that this moment, *this very second*, is the new exact low point of my life.

"No, Beth," I say through gritted teeth, "I don't want you to ask Parker if he can give me a ride to school."

"Okay," she says, standing up and evidently deciding

her sisterly duties have been fulfilled for the year. "Well, I tried."

She bounds out of the room, oblivious as ever.

There's another enormous thunderclap, and now the rain is starting to fall.

I can't sleep.

I've checked the stove, I've peed a million times, I've rubbed one out, but I still can't sleep. This is the biggest thunderstorm I've ever heard and rain is pounding on the roof. But that's not what's keeping me up. My mind is just racing.

I decide to flip on the TV. Usually watching TV doesn't help me fall asleep, but I'm willing to try anything. I flip through the channels, but it's the middle of the night and nothing is on. To make matters worse, some of the stations are all fuzzy, probably because of the storm.

I stop on Skinemax. Much to my surprise, it's coming in completely clear. Ironically, the storm seems to have unblocked it. It's my lucky night (yes, this is now what I consider "luck"). I have no idea what corny movie I'm watching, so I press the Info button on the remote. On-screen it reads:

Sensual Moon IV **(premiere)—The forbidden tale of a man with mysterious,**

erotic powers. Rated TV-MA. Contains
nudity and explicit sexual activity.

Sensual Moon IV? Man, they really must be churning
these movies out because I've still never seen *II* or *III.* I'm
about to grab my phone from my nightstand and text Steve
to make sure he knows it's on, but then I remember we
don't talk anymore. It really sucks. I'm sure he's watching
anyway, but that's little consolation.

I settle in to watch as the rain intensifies. Like the first
film I saw in this epic saga, *Sensual Moon IV* is basically
about a guy who gets laid a lot, and features tons of gratu-
itous nudity. As near as I can tell in this one, the main
character's "mysterious, erotic power" is that he can blow
women's clothes clean off with just one touch. In the very
first scene, a real estate lady is showing him around a
mansion. He touches her sleeve and suddenly her clothes
fly off and she's completely naked.

Let's just say I never make it past the first scene. I turn
the TV off and turn the light on my nightstand on. I open
the drawer and take out my beat-off sheet. It's time to
record my second wank of the night. As I make the tally,
I notice the bottle of Lexapro that's still in the drawer.
It's almost completely full since I had just gotten the
prescription refilled before I decided to stop taking it.
I look at the bottle and then at the pathetic sheet in
my hand filled with tallies. I look at the bottle, then back
at the sheet. Bottle then sheet, bottle then sheet, bottle
then sheet. Then I do something completely unexpected.
Something that only crosses my consciousness for a

brief second, but that I decide to act on before it's too late.

I rip up the sheet.

I take that growing stack of Post-it notes and rip it to shreds. I tear them and I tear them until each piece is too small to tear again. I tear them until I can't tell which tally is which. I tear them until there's no way I can ever tape them back together again.

I sit on the edge of my bed, holding the tiny scraps of paper in my trembling hands. Seventeen months of "work" literally torn to shreds. I expect to feel regret or anxiety. But I don't. Instead, I feel . . . *liberated*. I feel encouraged. I feel emboldened.

As the rain continues to hammer down on the roof above me, I consider my options: I can remain a slave to my bizarre compulsions forever, or I can sack up and actually *do something* about it. I can be a better friend to Steve, I can win Amy back, and I can show everyone I've changed. But I can't half-ass it. I need to go for broke.

There's just no way I can leave high school like the doormat I was when I started. I can't let the girl of my dreams and my best friend in the world just move on without me. And I sure as hell can't stay home *jerking off and counting it* while life goes on without me.

I don't know if it's the insomnia or the loneliness or the frustration or what. But something just flips in my brain, like the neuron that connected my red Cons to anger. Maybe it's that I've got nothing to lose. But whatever it is, right here and now, with my boxers still around my ankles, I decide that I have one last chance to prove everyone wrong.

I may be strange, but I'm no loser. I can handle whatever the world throws at me. *I know I can; I have to.*

My name is Chuck. I'm seventeen years old. And OCD be damned, I'm going camping.

HHT HHT HHT
HHT HHT HHT
HHT HHT HHT
HHT III

The Greulichs' garage is damp and musty and I'm trying to get out of here as quickly as possible. They *do* have a lot of camping gear, though most of it looks like it hasn't been used since the Greulichs were my age, which was possibly over a hundred years ago. They're also standing over me, creeping me out. I grab a tent, a sleeping bag, some other random shit, then wave halfheartedly and haul ass outta there.

The afternoon air is cool as I walk the twenty or so feet back to my house. It just stopped raining a little while ago but it's still misty out. Doesn't matter; I'm determined. I'm going on this trip no matter what. There's no turning back.

I get home and spread everything out on the floor in my bedroom. I'm just starting to pack when Mom comes in. I told Beth this morning that I was going (and that I'd drive myself, thank you very much), but I haven't told Mom and Dad. This is gonna be interesting.

"Beth tells me you're going on the camping trip," Mom says.

"Yup."

"You? You're going camping?"

"That's right."

"Are you sure this is a good idea?"

"It's fine for Beth to go but not me?"

I briefly consider blowing up Beth's spot and telling Mom that it's not a school-sanctioned trip and no adults are gonna be there. But I decide it's not worth the hassle.

"Well," Mom says, briefly stymied by my challenge, "Beth doesn't have a problem with . . . you know . . ."

"Grass? Bugs? Dirt?" I ask.

"Exactly."

"I know, Mom. But I have to do this. I'll be okay."

"I'm sure you will be, but I just don't know why you want to put yourself through this."

"This thing is a big deal. Everyone from school is gonna be there."

"Is this about Amy and Steve?"

Mom: always right.

"Yeah it's about Amy and Steve. I want to hang out with them."

"But I thought they weren't talking to you."

"And how is *not* going gonna fix that?"

Mom senses we've hit a wall and it's time to change tactics.

"Dad is gonna be home soon. I'm sure he'll want to say goodbye."

I give up trying to roll the sleeping bag up nicely and just start jamming it into its sack.

"Mom, I'm gonna be back tomorrow, he doesn't need to say goodbye."

Nice try, though.

"Chuck," Mom says, crossing her arms, "you're behaving erratically. It's making me nervous."

"Mom, I'm actually behaving the *opposite* of erratic. I'm behaving normal. This is what kids do. They go camping with everyone else. Why can't I just be normal for once?"

"Because you *aren't* normal, sweetheart."

I look at her, a little offended.

"Not in a bad way," she continues. "You're an incredible son. But you're just different."

I know what Mom is trying to say. OCD kids who stop taking their meds shouldn't run to do the one thing that sets them off the most. But she doesn't understand that I know what I'm doing.

"Mom, do you want your 'incredible son' to be holed up inside for the rest of his life? I need to get out. Besides, the campsite is only like two miles away. Nothing is gonna happen."

This argument fails to dispel the worried look on her face.

"I'm gonna call Dad again," she says, and hurries out of the room.

She can call Dad all she wants, but nothing is gonna stop me today.

I continue searching my room, making sure I've got everything I need. I come across the bottle of Lexapro and decide to pack it. I figure if things get really messy it won't hurt to take one. I also find a flashlight as well as a travel bottle of hand sanitizer—perfect for the crazy person on the go.

I hear a honk and look out my bedroom window. I spy

Beth getting into Parker's truck and them taking off to-gether. I picture my classmates driving to the campgrounds from all around town—cars full of anticipation and beer. I look at the sky. The sun is just beginning to peek out from behind the clouds.

ocking brown Cons, though I'm not sure if I actually feel confident or if it's just wishful thinking.

I pull up to the Randall Kaufman campgrounds in West Lake in Mom's car. She spent another hour trying to talk me out of it and stalling before I finally convinced her it was okay to let me go. Luckily, I got out of the house before Dad got home so they didn't have a chance to gang up on me.

It's about six o'clock when I finally get to the parking lot, so most of the class has already been here for a couple of hours. I can see our campsite in the distance: it's basically just a clearing surrounded by heavy woods on three sides. There's a bonfire going in the center. From where I'm parked, I can vaguely make out laughter and good-natured yelling. I take a deep breath and get out of the car.

My quasi-confidence is shattered as soon as I take one step on the ground. *I'm an idiot.* Never in a million years did it cross my mind what effect last night's storm would have on the campgrounds. My left Con sinks into the mud. The white stripe around the sole is now the same color brown as the rest of my sneaker. I have a fleeting sense of despair and pause on the precipice between getting back in the car and forging ahead. I force myself to put my right Con in the mud as well. I grimace as I close the car door behind me. I continue.

I grab all of my gear from the trunk, press the Lock button on Mom's electronic keychain about twenty times until the car alarm beeps just right, and then make my way toward the festivities.

The grass is soaking wet, which is good in a way because it sort of cleans off my sneakers. But I'm struck with a sudden foreboding about what condition the campsite itself is gonna be in. It really rained like a motherfucker last night. I keep going. One Con in front of the other.

It's still light out, so as I get closer, I can start to make out details. Some of the meatheads have their shirts off and are chasing each other around the fire, cans of beer in hand. There's a variety of tents set up, in all shapes and sizes, none of which look as shitty as mine. A few couples are making out. There are several iPods playing at once, competing for attention so that I can't distinguish any individual songs.

As I approach the outer ring of tents, I notice that the grass here has almost completely disintegrated. I'm guessing it's a combination of all the foot traffic and the storm—the campsite is now nothing but mud. There's mud on the tips of the logs in the bonfire, there's mud on some of the tents, and there's mud all over the drunk kids' clothes. My pulse quickens.

I find an empty patch toward the back of the site, on the edge of the woods, and decide it's as good a place as any. I'd rather be isolated than in the middle of the mayhem. I yank a small plastic tarp out of my bag and the smell instantly transports me back to the Greulichs' mothbally garage. It's strangely comforting. I manage to put the tarp down on the mud and throw my gear on top. I'm sweating, my sneakers are filthy, and my hands are shaking. But I'm alive.

I survey my surroundings. About fifty feet to my left I see Ashley, who has the biggest tent of anyone because he's the tallest guy ever. Next to him are Stacey and Wendy. They have matching hot pink tents that look like they have built-in, like, *porches* attached to the front. Their tents are nicer than my bedroom. I despise them now more than ever.

My seething is disrupted, though, when I realize Amy is nowhere to be found. Surely if she's here, she'd be with one of those three people. This is simultaneously encouraging and discouraging. *Nothing is ever simple.*

Next to Stacey and Wendy are my sister and Parker. Parker's tent is red and stupid. Beth, who got to the Greulichs' first, has a slightly less shitty version of my tent. I'm relieved she actually bothered to set hers up and not just crash in Parker's. There's a pile of empty beer cans next to Parker's tent. He finishes another one and then burps. My sister giggles like an idiot.

Across the site, on the other side of the fire, I spot Kanha. He's wearing a do-rag. I crack a smile. What a moron. Next to him are the Barrys, who, if I'm not mistaken, are looking at a textbook. I assume they're preparing—during Senior

Weekend no less—for their climactic final mathletic competition. I silently declare myself superior to them and that makes me feel an iota better.

I look past the Barrys and suddenly find myself making eye contact with Steve. He stares at me from across the campsite, a look of astonishment on his face. I don't blame him. I'm literally the last person he should expect to see here. I quickly look away, only able to guess what he's thinking.

My tent goes up a lot easier than I expected (then again, I always expect the worst). I throw the rest of my shit inside, then sit with my ass in the tent and my feet sticking out onto the tarp.

Reality quickly sets in: without the distraction of getting my gear from the car to the campsite, or setting up the tarp and the tent, I'm forced to soak in the severity of my situation. I'm surrounded by mud. My sneakers, socks, and hands are caked with it. There's dirt and blades of grass *inside* the tent. Mosquitoes buzz everywhere. My face is sticky with sweat. I spot one rickety porta-potty in the distance.

You proved your point. Amy's not even here. Just go home.

I close my eyes tightly, then reopen them. I'm starting to get itchy. Really, really itchy.

I think I'm gonna hyperventilate. That is, until I'm distracted once again.

Parker has gotten up and is making his way toward Steve.

arker, stop!"

Beth is yelling at Parker, who is stomping across the campsite in Steve's direction. Parker is definitely drunk—he almost stumbles into the fire as he marches past it (which, honestly, would have been the greatest thing ever). Parker is about ten feet away when Steve finally realizes what's happening. I can sense Steve's heart sink when he spots Parker charging at him. Without thinking, I get up and head toward Steve as well.

"Hey, Fudge Packer! What the fuck are you doing here?"

Parker is kind of slurring, which worries me. Who knows what he'll do?

Steve doesn't speak; he just stands there with his hands out, as if to say, "It doesn't really matter how I respond, does it?"

"Come on, you fucking *nerd*. Say something!"

Parker has stopped about three feet in front of Steve. I arrive and stand off to the side. Beth is behind Parker, continuing to yell at him.

"Parker, just leave him alone!"

Parker turns around and yells back at her: "Will you shut up?"

"Hey," Steve says, before I even have a chance to react, "don't talk to her like that!"

Parker relishes the challenge. "Oh yeah? What are you gonna do about it, Fudge Packer?"

Unsurprisingly, a crowd has already gathered—with Parker and Steve at the center and me and Beth just steps away from them. The entire class huddles around the four of us in a bloodthirsty circle. I can't hear music anymore, just random yelling from bystanders—some supporting Parker, fewer supporting Steve, and most, it seems, just wanting some action of any kind.

"Fight!" someone yells out, whipping the crowd into a frenzy.

Beth walks up behind Parker and grabs his arm. "Let's go!"

Parker roughly yanks his arm out of her grasp—definitely more forceful than necessary.

I take a step closer, sensing the irony of getting pulverized to defend the sister who I hate.

"Hey! Don't touch her!" Steve yells.

And then, to everyone's disbelief, Steve walks right up to Parker and pushes *him*.

The crowd lets out a big "Ohhhh!"

Parker barely moves an inch, though, and is now standing face-to-face with Steve, towering over him and grinning like a wild man.

Steve struggles to maintain his composure.

Parker clenches his right fist.

My body moves without permission from my brain.

I dash toward Parker and Steve.

I position myself in between them, facing Parker.

I've placed myself in the middle of the storm.

"Chuck, no!" Beth yells.

Steve is speechless.

"What the *fuck* are you doing?" Parker snarls at me.

"Just walk away, Parker," I say. It feels like someone else is talking.

For a brief second, Parker seems to relent, as if he's grown bored with us. Then, he takes a step forward and pushes me into Steve. We both stumble backwards a few steps like a couple of circus clowns. Steve still doesn't say anything to me. A hush falls over the crowd. I attempt to reason with the beast.

"Parker, why are—"

It happens in slow motion. I can see Parker's right fist flying at my left eye, but am powerless to do anything about it. Just before the punch hits my face, everything goes silent, like when your ears clog on an airplane.

THWAP!

Next thing I know, I'm on the ground. There's mud in my mouth, on my tongue, and all over my clothes. I put my hand over my eye, but I don't feel pain. I think I'm in shock. I can't stand up.

When I get my bearings, I see that Parker still has his fist cocked and Steve is still standing there, helpless.

"Are you ready for some of that, huh?" Parker taunts.

Steve puts his hands out again as if surrendering.

Sunset is approaching, and from my vantage point on the ground, I can just make out the moon on the horizon. It's nearly full.

A light bulb goes off in my head. A great, big, amazing light bulb.

"Steve!" I yell. "Steve!"

Steve has more important things to worry about. Parker is chomping at the bit.

"*Steve!*"

He finally turns to me.

"Did you see *Sensual Moon IV* last night?" I ask.

"What?" Steve looks at me like I have three heads.

"*Sensual Moon IV*. On Skinemax. Did you see it?"

Steve, perhaps assuming I've suffered severe brain damage from the punch, turns back to Parker, who's cracking his knuckles in anticipation of bashing two losers in one night.

"*Steve!*" I yell again.

"Yes," he says finally, "I fucking saw it!"

"You have the power!" I say.

"What?"

"You have the power!" I repeat, pointing at Parker.

In this moment, nearly a decade of best friendship comes to fruition. All those sleepovers, all those Facebook chats, all those inside jokes, they've forged a bond between me and Steve that is paying off right now. A look of understanding washes over Steve's face. My idea is transferred to his brain. He smirks almost imperceptibly.

Steve steps toward Parker, who is seemingly dumbfounded by Steve's sudden boldness. Before Parker can throw a punch, Steve reaches in, grabs the waistband of Parker's warm-up pants, and in one fluid motion rips them clean off, the snaps running down Parker's legs opening simultaneously.

Steve finds himself with his arm raised triumphantly, clutching Parker's pants in his hand. Parker is left standing in front of the entire senior class wearing a raggedy pair of tighty whiteys.

The laughter comes quickly and loudly from the crowd. Waves and waves of it raining down on the humiliated Parker. Steve looks at me and I look back at him, not really knowing what to do next. Success is not a familiar feeling for either of us.

"Fudge Packer!"

Uh oh. Parker has gathered himself and, despite being half-naked in front of the jeering crowd, sets his sights on revenge. He sneers at Steve so angrily that the throng begins to quiet. Steve drops the warm-up pants. I finally get back on my feet. And that's when Steve does something so strange, so bizarre, he's the only person on earth who would ever think of it.

Steve starts pumping his fists out in front him, first slowly, then faster, then as quickly as he possibly can. Left, right, left, right, left, right, left, right. Only I realize what's he's doing.

Wii Boxing.

Parker and the crowd are equally perplexed but Steve keeps pumping away. Finally ready to dispatch him for good, Parker takes a few half steps toward Steve to gather some momentum and winds up to deliver the punch of all punches. Parker plants his lead foot but—either because of all the mud or just too many beers—slips and hurtles headfirst at Steve. Parker's face meets one of Steve's flying fists and CRACK!

Parker wobbles for a second, then crumples facedown in the mud, the back of his tighty whiteys exposed for the world to see. The crowd erupts in cheers.

Steve Sludgelacker just knocked his nemesis out cold.

After cheering Steve's victory, the crowd loses interest and disperses. Steve, who's not used to so much attention, seems more relieved than anything. Parker starts to come to as Ashley is wrapping a towel around him. He lifts Parker up and helps him stumble woozily back to his tent. Neither Parker nor Ashley looks back in Steve's direction.

I'm still struggling to get the dirt out of my mouth when Steve approaches me. He looks a little dazed.

"You okay?" I ask.

"I think so," he says. "How's your eye?"

I reach up and touch it. It's tender, but to be honest there's so much mud I can't even tell if it's swollen or not.

"It's fine I guess."

"That was pretty crazy, huh?" he says. "Did that really just happen?"

"Yeah, it did," I respond, equally amazed. "Listen, Steve. I'm sorry."

"You don't have to apologize."

"No, I think I do. I'm sorry I didn't help you out sooner. That was really selfish of me."

"Well . . . better late than never, right?" Steve jokes.

"Something like that," I say. "I was wrapped up in so much shit. I guess I just took our friendship for granted. I'll never do that again. You know, if you still want to be friends or whatever."

Steve grins. Then he hugs me.

"I'll always be your friend, man," he says. Then he looks at all the mud that's rubbed off on him. "What the . . . Chuck, you're fucking gross."

"I know." It concerns me that this hasn't sunk in yet.

"I'm sorry I talked all that shit to you," Steve says.

"Don't worry about it."

"Thanks for having my back tonight," he adds.

"I can't believe you knocked Parker out," I say.

"I know, right? My fist kinda hurts. Is that normal?"

"I have no idea," I admit.

"I couldn't have done it without you, Chuck."

"Steve," I say, "that was all you. *You* did it. I mean, Wii Boxing? Come on!"

"I told you: natural talent, Chuck. Natural talent."

We both laugh.

"By the way," Steve says, "how did you know I watched *Sensual Moon IV*?"

"I don't know; I just did."

"Have you seen II yet?"

"No, I haven't."

"Oh, you gotta—"

"I know, Steve, it's the best one."

We share another laugh. It feels great to be friends with Steve again. I think we're gonna be talking about this night for a long time.

A mosquito bites me. I slap my arm, leaving a handprint of mud. My eye is starting to throb a bit. I try to focus.

"So," Steve says, "there is one thing I've been meaning to tell you for a while now. You know that story I'm always telling about my hand job?"

I shake my head, knowing at long last he's going to admit he's full of shit.

"All true," he says with a huge smile. "All true."

"Fuck you!" I joke.

I playfully push him, and then we hug again. Then I notice someone standing behind Steve.

"I think someone wants to talk to you," I say.

It's Beth. She walks up to him.

"Hi, Steve."

"Hi."

"I just wanted to, you know, thank you sticking up for me back there."

"Oh, it's okay. He just seemed a little drunk is all," Steve says.

Steve's adrenaline must still be pumping because he's actually forming coherent sentences.

"Yeah, well Parker is a big jerk," Beth says. "It was really brave of you to stand up to him like that."

I think Steve is blushing.

"I just did what I had to do," he says.

"I guess I'll see you later," Beth continues. "I'm gonna go move my tent away from that douche bag."

"Do you need a hand?" Steve asks, remarkably poised.

Just when I think Beth is about to blow him off once again, she relents. "Sure," she shrugs, "that'd be great."

Steve looks at me. I refuse to explicitly give my blessing, so I just do an awful job of pretending I'm not paying attention.

Steve and Beth both smile at me. Then they walk back to Beth's tent together. I stand there long enough to see them start to chat.

I head back to my own tent. As I do, I unexpectedly get a few passing words of encouragement from my classmates.

"Nice job, Chuck!"

"Good work, man!"

"Fuck Parker!"

"You're the real G, dog! You're the real G!"

Besides Kanha, most of these people I haven't spoken to since we were in Plainville Elementary. It feels good, but a few slaps on the back can't hide what I've been fighting since I stepped in the mud in the parking lot: all of my OCD "things" are being triggered at once and I'm not sure how much longer I can handle it.

I get back to my tent and worry I'm beginning to experience sensory overload. I can feel the mud and sweat and bug bites on my skin. It smells like burning logs, wet grass, and the Greulichs' garage. I can hear crickets chirping deep in the woods as the sun begins to set. I can taste dirt on my lips. My eye is definitely starting to swell.

I collapse onto my tarp. I reach into the bag in my tent and grab the travel sanitizer. I squirt the entire contents onto my hands. I rub them like crazy. It just seems to be pushing the dirt around. I try to rub some on my face. *Ow!* It stings right where I got punched.

Everyone else is having a blast.

I, on the other hand, am having a panic attack.

IIII IIII IIII
IIII IIII IIII
IIII IIII IIII
IIII IIII II

I'm huddled inside my tent, jamming stuff from my backpack into my pockets in case I need to make a run for it and ditch the camping gear. I'm not thinking straight at all. There's dirt buried deep under my fingernails and I can't get it out. The inside of the tent is completely muddy now, so I have no safe haven. I don't want to be here anymore.

I crawl out of my tent to see if I can squeeze any more sanitizer out of the bottle I discarded. And that's when I see her in the dying light: Amy.

She's standing with Stacey and Wendy. I'm nowhere near close enough to be able to hear what they're saying, but I can see Amy is wearing flip-flops, shorts, and a tank top. It's been a while since I got a chance to really look at her. I miss it.

I have no idea how long she's been at the campsite or if she saw me take that punch, but I pray she did. I'm scratching my arms and legs nonstop. I feel contaminated. I realize that Amy is gonna see me in shambles—dirty and acting insane. That's the exact opposite reason I came out here. She can't see me like this. All *weird*. But it's only a matter of time.

I scurry around to the back of the tarp, behind my tent, so that I'm hidden from view. I sit with my knees pulled up against my chest. I can't leave and risk seeing Amy, but I can't stay here. I rock back and forth like a crazy person. I think I hear people walking in my direction. It might be Amy, it might not be. There's only one place to go.

I take off running into the woods. I run straight back from the campsite, though after about twenty feet I have no idea which direction is which. Branches and bushes are scraping me as I run by. I can hear my own breath. I trip on a log, roll on the ground, then get up and keep going. I run and run and run. Soon I can't hear any sounds from the campsite or see any glimmer from the bonfire and I have no idea how to get back there.

I keep running, escaping from everything. I almost run headfirst into a tree, but I keep going. I run through a puddle and feel it splash up into my face. I keep going. I'm running from everything I *can't* do—be normal, hang out, have fun. I'm running from everything I *can't* be—a boyfriend, sane, a human being. I run and run and run.

I'm lost. I'm out of breath. It's getting dark.

I lie down in the middle of the woods and have a breakdown. I roll around in the mud and the muck and the shit. I grab clumps of leaves and rub them into my hair. I wipe my face with the dirt from my hands. Everything I hate most in life is all over me. For a minute it feels weird—I think "cathartic" is the word. I'm released from my compulsions.

My triggers overrun my body. There's nothing I can do to reduce the anxiety so I just let it wash over me. I'm free.

And then I'm not. The gravity of the situation hits me like a thousand thunderclaps. *I'll never be clean again.*

I can't leave the woods. I can barely move. I get on my hands and knees. I start to cry. Thick, salty tears. Tears that merge with snot and roll down my dirty cheeks and mix with the mud. It's too much. *I can't fix this.*

I puke. It feels awful. It smells. It makes my eye hurt worse. It feels like it's gonna burst out of its socket.

I puke again. This time not much comes out. It burns my throat. I can't stop crying. *I don't want to be here anymore.*

I reach into my pocket, hoping there's a tissue, a napkin, a piece of paper, a To Do list, *anything* I can use to wipe my face. My fingers grasp a familiar plastic bottle.

I take it out of my pocket. It's just barely light enough to read:

PLAINVILLE PHARMACY
DR. SRINIVASAN, AHLADITA

TAYLOR, CHARLES
TAKE ONE TABLET DAILY
LEXAPRO

I'm still crying. I try to open the bottle. I can't get it open. My hands are too wet and dirty. And it's childproof. One final insult.

I finally get it open. I pour everything into my disgusting hand. There's probably like twenty pills.

I wonder what would happen if I take them all. I wonder *if* I can take them all—I don't even have any water.

I think about my school locker and my parents' stove and the elevator button in Dr. S.'s office—stupid, inanimate objects that haunt my very existence.

I stare at the pills in my hand. It's come to this.

My leg is wet. It's the mud or the puke or something.

I stare at the pills.

Something wet is *touching* my leg.

I just stare.

Something is fucking licking my leg.

I look back. I do a double take.

I see the most amazing, astonishing, bewildering sight I've ever laid eyes on.

I can't believe it.

It's Buttercup.

I look at her and she looks at me. I think I might be hallucinating.

She barks.

I recognize that bark.

I think she recognizes me.

She leaps into my arms and starts licking my face. Some OCD trumps other OCD once again because her tongue actually feels *good*.

I check the tag on her collar. It's scratched up and caked with dirt. I turn it over.

Amy's phone number is on the back. It's Buttercup all right. She looks skinny and grimy but otherwise okay. She doesn't look hurt or anything. She must have been wandering around for weeks; we're not that far from Amy's house.

I've honestly never been more excited to see an animal in my entire life. I rub her neck and ears like I've seen Amy do.

I realize I'm still clutching all the pills tightly in one hand. I manage to dump them back into the bottle, dirt and all, and shove the bottle back into my pocket. As I do, I realize I've been carrying a flashlight the whole time.

Buttercup runs in a circle around me, alternating between barking, sniffing, and licking. I stand up and she starts jumping up and down, pawing at my waist. I pick her up. I've never voluntarily held a dog before.

It's time for both of us to go home.

Even with the flashlight, it's so dark that I start to worry I'll never get out of the woods. But after several wrong turns, I finally hear the faint sounds of Senior Weekend in the distance. I'm able to follow the noise back to my original path from the campsite. I clutch Buttercup tightly, though I highly doubt she's going anywhere.

When I emerge from the woods, I notice the bonfire is twice as big as when I left. The entire campsite is glowing. As soon as I get near enough to see anything, Steve spots me and points.

"There he is!" he yells.

Beth and Kanha look relieved. I'm just surprised anyone even noticed I was gone.

Then I hear what can only be described as a cry of joy. It's Amy. She sees me and Buttercup and comes running toward us.

She reaches me just as I get to the outer ring of tents, Steve, Beth, and Kanha following closely behind.

"Buttercup!" she cries.

I hand Amy the dog and she clutches it close to her chest.

"How did you . . . where did you . . ." she sputters.

"She was just wandering around back there."

After checking to make sure Buttercup is uninjured, Amy suddenly gives me a great big hug.

She smells so clean.

"Thank you, thank you, thank you, Chuck," she says into my ear.

She takes a step back and looks me up and down. I must look like a train wreck. Amy is filthy just from hugging me.

"What happened to you? Are you okay?"

"Yeah, I'm fine. I just went for a walk and got a little lost."

"We were worried about you," Steve chimes in.

"I'm okay, I swear. Go have fun. Seriously, go. It's cool."

Satisfied that I'm in one piece and in good hands, Steve, Beth, and Kanha head back to the bonfire, leaving me and Amy alone.

Amy can't stop stroking Buttercup and rubbing her nose against the dog's.

"Thank you so much, Chuck."

"I'm just glad she's okay."

Amy smiles and hugs me again with Buttercup still in her arms.

"Oh, Chuck. I can't believe you found her. I can't believe . . . you *came* here."

"I guess," I stammer, suddenly at a loss for words, "I guess I came here for you. To show you I could do it."

A single tear drops from Amy's eye. I don't know if this is a good thing or a bad thing.

"Amy, I just want to say I'm sorry again for—"

"No. Don't."

"No?"

"Chuck, I'm the one who owes you an apology."

"You do?"

"I should have been more understanding about what you were—what you *are* going through."

"It's okay . . ."

"No, listen, Chuck. When you needed me most, I wasn't there for you. I wasn't a good friend, even though you've been nothing short of amazing. I promise I'll make it up to you. *I'm* the one who's sorry."

There's a lump in my throat.

"You're all dirty" is all I can manage to say.

"And who's fault is that?" she quips.

I shrug playfully.

"There's one more thing," she says. "I'm so, so, so sorry that I brought Buttercup into your room that day. I should have asked first. Otherwise none of this would have ever happened."

"Well, he *is* a little messy," I admit.

"She."

Damn it. Still always screw that up.

"Right, she."

"I'm so glad you found her. I'm so glad you're *here*."

"I did it for you, Amy."

"No, Chuck. You did it for *you*."

"What do you mean?"

"Look at yourself," Amy says. "You're camping! You just held a dog. You're . . . disgusting. But you're doing it. Me,

Steve, we're all just along for the ride. This is the Chuck Taylor show. You're the one who made it happen. Now you can do anything. I'm so proud of you."

She hugs me again. It feels *right*.

"Chuck," she says, her face nuzzled in my chest.

"Yeah?"

"You stink."

I laugh. "I know."

Buttercup barks with delight.

"So does *she* by the way."

Amy gives Buttercup's fur a sniff then holds her up to her face. "P. U.!"

Buttercup responds by licking her.

"Hey, Amy," I say, "there's something I need to tell you."

"Anything."

It's time to come out with it already.

"I hate calculus."

"What?"

"I hate math. *Hate* it. I'm good at it, but I hate it. I only told you I liked it 'cause, I don't know, you're so cool and I didn't know what else to say when you asked me to tutor you."

"Chuck, you don't give yourself enough credit. You're like the coolest guy I know."

"Come on . . ."

"It's true. You're so funny, and so nice, and you're such a great brother and a great friend."

Every time Amy says something nice about me, I fall for her all over again.

"Wait," I say, "why do you think I'm such a great brother and a great friend?"

"You stood up to the biggest bully in school."

"You saw that?"

"Uh huh."

"You saw me get punched in the face?"

"Yup," Amy smirks.

I study her expression. She's telling the truth.

"Pretty cool, huh?"

"Pretty cool," Amy echoes. "By the time I finally got the nerve to come over and see how you were doing, you were gone."

It's probably better that way.

"How's your eye?"

"It stings a little."

She brushes some of the mud and dirt away from my face.

"Let's get outta here, get you cleaned up, and find some ice."

She smiles and I can't help but smile back.

"Right on," I say.

HH HH LH
HH HH LH
LH HH HH
LH HH IIII

I stare in the bathroom mirror. This time, I'm not the least bit concerned about my cheekbones.

It's taken a couple of weeks, but any remnants of my black eye are finally gone. The timing could not be better.

My dad's hands reach around my neck, adjusting my bow tie.

"Looking sharp," Dad says. "You clean up nice."

I have to admit, I *do* look good in a tux.

"Dad," I say, "I was thinking maybe this week, when a game is on, you can teach me a little about basketball. I want to start learning."

"Chuck," Dad says, grasping my shoulders, "the season ended yesterday."

"Oh."

"But how about next season, when you're home from college, we *go* to a game?"

"That'd be great," I say.

Dad smiles at me via the mirror.

When you're home from college. It sounds so strange.

"Mom, it's fine!" Beth shouts.

She's standing next to me in our bathroom, in a dress, as Mom fixes her hair.

The prospect of Beth also going to prom doesn't thrill me in the slightest but, quite frankly, nothing can bring me down tonight.

"Hey, Beth," I say, "thanks for finally accepting my friend request. Took you long enough."

I'm preparing for an onslaught of snarkiness, but before Beth can retort, the doorbell rings. Beth remains silent. It's the nicest thing she's ever said to me.

"Ray, can you get the door?" Mom says. "It's probably for Beth."

My dad goes downstairs.

"Both of you look so nice," Mom gushes.

"Yeah, yeah," Beth says, as she scurries out of the bathroom before Mom can make any more adjustments.

It's just me and Mom now.

"Are you excited for tonight?" she asks.

"I'm really excited."

Mom just looks at me proudly.

"That's it? No more questions?" I ask.

"Nope," she says, "no more questions."

She kisses me on the forehead and leaves.

I come downstairs a few minutes later to find Beth and Steve taking pictures together. Beth dwarfs him in her high heels, but somehow they look okay together. Steve looks good in his tux, too. He seems physically unable to wipe the smile off his face.

"You look handsome," Beth says to Steve. It's the first

time I've ever perceived her to be, well, acting awkwardly. I kept my distance when they started hanging out after Senior Weekend but, hell, she must actually like him.

"I need to get my purse," Beth says. "I'll be right back." She scoots away.

"Let's get a picture of the two dashing young men," Mom says.

Me and Steve stand next to each other, attempting to hold a smile while Mom tries to figure out how to operate the camera on her phone. "Say cheese!"

She takes the picture.

That's a keeper.

"I'm gonna see if Beth needs any help," Mom says. She goes back upstairs too.

Dad approaches Steve.

"Home by midnight, understand?"

"Yes, Mr. Taylor."

Dad pats Steve on the back, maybe a little too hard.

"I'll be in the kitchen," he says, and walks out of the room.

I turn to my best friend.

"You joined Mathletes, entered a competition, and won . . ."

"That's right," he says.

"And you still couldn't meet any other girls to take to prom besides my sister?"

Steve shakes his head. "Let's just say the female mathletes don't quite have Beth's . . . *variables.*"

"Steve, what did I say about talking about my sister? I *will* kill you."

Steve laughs. "I'm just kidding! You know I'll take good care of her."

He's right. If there's anyone on the planet I trust, it's good ol' Steve.

"By the way," he says, digging into his tux pocket, "here."

He hands me a five-dollar bill.

"What's this?"

"I owe you five bucks, remember? From that time with Parker in the hallway?"

"Come on, Steve."

"Nope, a debt's a debt. Take it."

"How about this?" I say, refusing payment. "Double or nothing Kanha throws up at prom."

"Deal," Steve says, smiling.

We shake on it.

After Steve and Beth leave, I retreat to my bedroom to fix my tux shoes, which are rubbing my feet like crazy. While there, I realize what time it is and take a bottle of Lexapro from my drawer. I swallow a pill with a swig of water, just like I do every day at this time. I put the Lexapros back in my drawer and the water bottle back down on my desk, right next to a To Do list with only one entry:

Dr. S.: Tuesdays at 3 pm

I sit down on my bed and am fiddling with my shoes again when I hear a knock. The door opens and in strolls Amy.

She looks gorgeous. I mean drop-dead, supermodel gorgeous. Her dress, her freckles, everything looks perfect. Plus, I'm shocked to notice that her hair is . . . well, *up*. Her bangs are out of her eyes for the very first time. Getting to see more of her face is almost too much for me to handle.

I'm stunned. It occurs to me that the wish I made on my eyelash all those months ago came true: I'm going to the prom with Amy.

I notice that she's carrying a box—a wrapped gift to be exact. For a moment, I have a flashback to the very first time Amy entered my room, carrying a box a bit squarer than this one. There were cupcakes inside. Thankfully, though, there's no Buttercup in tow this time. I quickly quash the memory of that fateful day—without knocking on wood.

"Amy," I say, "what are you doing here? I was just gonna get you as soon as I fix these stupid shoes."

"I know," she says, "but I wanted to surprise you."

Classic Amy, operating by her own rules. It never gets old.

She walks in and sits down next to me on my bed, never acknowledging the box in her hands.

"You look beautiful," I say, "and totally not corporate at all."

"Aww, thanks. You don't look so bad yourself."

Amy must find it amusing how easily she can make me blush.

"So," she says, nonchalantly crossing her legs, which momentarily scrambles my brain, "that day in Calc, when I had to go to the blackboard and correct the answer you got wrong . . . why were you so nervous?"

I have no idea what she's talking about.

"Huh?"

"That day, when you blurted out 'You're pretty.'"

Of course I remember that day, but what is she *talking about?*

"You were wearing yellow Cons. That means you were nervous, right?"

I just sit there, slack-jawed. *Has Amy figured out what I think she's figured out?*

"You wear yellow Cons when you're nervous, right? You were wearing them that day. And then any other time we had a big test you weren't sure about, you also wore them."

No one in the universe knows about my system, not even Steve. I've never written the code down anywhere or ever uttered a word about it to anyone, including Dr. S. It's the only thing I won't use CBT on. It's my *thing*.

I'm so astonished, it's hard to form words. A part of me is still convinced Amy just took a lucky guess.

"And when you wear the pink ones—which are rad by the way—that's bored, right? I noticed that any day you complained about being bored, you were wearing pink Cons."

She figured it out.

"And orange, that's—"

"Tired," we say in unison.

"Yeah," I manage. "How did you know?"

"How did I know what? That you wear a different color depending on your mood? I dunno, I guess just by paying attention to you."

Can I swoon now? Please?

"You have so many different pairs," she continues, "and nothing you do is ever random. I figured there had to be something to it. It was actually kinda fun to figure out."

Turns out, Amy knows me better than anyone.

"There is one thing I was wondering about, though," she says. "On my first day of school, you wore blue Cons. But you never wore them again."

"Wait a minute," I exclaim. "You *saw* me that day? That first day in Cimaglia?"

"Of course I did," she says, as if it's the most obvious thing in the world.

"I was excited because they were announcing Senior Weekend that morning," I explain.

"Ah," she says, "that makes sense."

Prom night has already exceeded my wildest expectations and we haven't even left my room yet.

"Should we go?" I say, tugging at my stupid tux shoes.

"In a second," Amy says, "but you won't be needing those shoes."

"What do you mean?"

She hands me the gift, which I'd forgotten all about.

"What is it?" I ask.

"Open it," she smirks.

Baffled, I tear open the wrapping paper. Inside is something I've seen countless times in my life: a Converse shoe box.

I look at Amy. She smiles.

I open the box and remove the tissue paper.

Underneath is a pair of brand-new high-top Chuck Taylor All Stars.

I hold them up. They're identical to every other pair in my collection, except for one major difference: they're not a solid color.

They're plaid.

"Amy," I say, overwhelmed with gratitude, "these are *awesome*."

"I'm glad you like them."

"But . . . what feeling should go with plaid?"

"Well," Amy says, "I think there's one you don't have covered yet."

She looks me in the eyes as I clutch the sneakers.

"Happy."

We kiss.

I can't wait to put them on.

lexaprosandcons.com

Acknowledgments

I'd like to thank my mom, dad, and sister, Caryn, for their perpetual support and guidance. They provided invaluable feedback upon reading the first draft of the book, which in essence can be summed up as "*Huh*, this actually isn't bad." Their love—and candor—knows no bounds, and for that I am eternally grateful.

My editor, Wes Adams, sparked to the plight of Chuck Taylor immediately and enabled me to bring him to life. The more bizarre and profane I wrote Chuck's character, the more enthusiastic Wes became—an attribute most authors can only hope for in an editor. His wisdom and tireless advocacy have been vital.

My agent Peter McGuigan and I are cut from the same cloth. We both love beer, broads, and books. He recognized the potential of *Lexapros and Cons* when it was nothing more than an outline, and shepherded it from proposal to paycheck. He and his team at Foundry Literary + Media are consummate professionals.

My attorney, Darren Trattner, has now seen me through a menagerie of books, scripts, and albums. Each contract is more sophisticated than the last, but Darren has remained committed to wringing the best possible deal for me no matter how lengthy or painful the process. Also, I'm legally obligated to say that.

You might not be holding this book in your hands had it not been for the efforts of Greg Galbraith, the Director of Marketing for Chuck Taylor All Star at Converse; and Elizabeth Fithian, the Director of Marketing, and Allison Verost, the Director of Publicity, at Macmillan Children's Publishing Group. Their contributions run as deep as their job titles are long.

Last but not least, a special thanks to all my fans around the world, who make every word worth writing.